WEST INDIAN SUMMER

WEST INDIAN SUMMER

The Test Series of 1988

PATRICK EAGAR and ALAN ROSS

HODDER AND STOUGHTON
LONDON SYDNEY AUCKLAND TORONTO

Dedication:
To Biddy

British Library Cataloguing in Publication Data

Eagar, Patrick
West Indian summer : the Test series of 1988.
1. England. Cricket. English teams. Test matches with
West Indian teams, 1988
I. Title   II. Ross, Alan, *1922–*
796.35′865

ISBN 0-340-49116-7

First published 1988

Published by Hodder and Stoughton,
a division of Hodder and Stoughton Ltd,
Mill Road, Dunton Green, Sevenoaks, Kent TN13 2YE
Editorial office: 47 Bedford Square, London WC1B 3DP

Photoset by Rowland Phototypesetting (London)Ltd

Printed and bound in Great Britain by Butler and Tanner Ltd
Frome and London

Book designed by Trevor Spooner

*Frontispiece – Marshall (left), Richardson and Dujon (behind) celebrate the
fall of Gooch's wicket – b Marshall 44 – in England's first innings at Lord's.*

Contents

Introduction

There was no shortage of prophets of doom about England's prospects for this West Indian summer. True, the West Indies had not distinguished themselves in the 1987 World Cup and they had only survived by the skin of their teeth against Pakistan at home, winning the third and final Test by only two wickets to draw the series. Earlier, on the last morning, they had looked certain losers against Imran Khan's enthusiastic team.

In contrast, England's Test record since demolishing the Australians in Australia during the winter of 1986-87 had been infinitely depressing. Only some inspired performances in one-day cricket, that took them to the World Cup Final in Calcutta, had interrupted a sequence as dismal in quality as it had been unsatisfactory in outcome. At home, during the summer of 1987, England had lost to New Zealand and Pakistan, and the dose was repeated by both those countries on their own grounds during the winter, resulting in England's longest barren period ever. Yet, curiously, West Indies, despite having successively walloped England 5-0 and 5-0 in the last two Test series, had only won one of the last seven one-day encounters between the two countries.

There was, then, some encouragement for England in the three one-day matches for the Texaco Trophy. Few people expected England to go down quite so limply in the Cornhill Tests as in the last two series, largely on the grounds of the comparative innocence of the new crop of West Indian fast bowlers, but even fewer predicted any serious reversal of form.

The weather during May 1988 had, on the whole, been kind. The first experiments with four-day county cricket had turned out unexpectedly well, several batsmen – Hick, Gooch, Gatting, Maynard, Fairbrother, Parker among them – running up large scores in circumstances usually denied them. Hick, in particular, carried almost everything before him, not only scoring 405 on one occasion, but threatening to reach 1000 runs in May quicker than anyone had achieved it before. In contrast, Gower and Botham scarcely made a run between them.

The West Indians quickly settled in. They may have had to share their last four successive Test series since beating England in the Caribbean – against Pakistan, twice,

New Zealand and India – but the ease with which they demolished Somerset and ran up a huge score against Sussex suggested they would suffer little for lack of acclimatisation. Richards himself had something to confirm in the ways of leadership. Now 36, his majesty and occasional disruptive ferocity as a batsman rather less often in evidence, it would be no small compensation were he to prove himself a mature, unifying, calm and successful captain. He had yet to prove himself to be all of these things.

The announcement of England's squad for the three one-day Internationals found no favour. Mike Selvey in *The Guardian* described the selections of Pringle and Athey as 'astounding' and the team as a whole 'a typical messy compromise between the captain's demands and selectorial whim.' The selection of Lynch Selvey assumed to be a mishearing of Gatting's request for lunch. John Thicknesse in *The Evening Standard* carried on his now familiar campaign against the selectors: 'Not by a long chalk for the first time in May's six years as chairman, selection of the squad was pitiful', Thicknesse's main cause for complaint was the preference for Athey over Gower: 'Gower does not need to be in form to be picked ahead of Athey, possessing such talent he can find it in a few minutes at the crease'. No-one found Botham's absence at all surprising, but Capel, his assumed replacement, was left out on grounds of fitness, despite having had a fine match for Northamptonshire following a knee operation. Despite almost unanimous opinion that Russell was technically the best wicket-keeper in the country and no mean batsman, Downton was again preferred to him. The two most successful and hostile fast bowlers of the moment, Agnew and Cowans, seemed scarcely to have been considered. Jarvis was out of action, so Dilley's partners would come from DeFreitas, Small and Radford, with Hemmings to share the spinning, if necessary, with Emburey. Three of England's party turned out to be West Indies born, Lynch, Small and DeFreitas, with two more coming from Africa, Lamb from the South and Radford from Zambia.

Gatting's day

Simmons has reason to look apprehensive, for Lamb is about to catch him. Once Haynes was fit, Simmons was bound to lose his place. He is an uninhibited striker of the ball, a batsman in the mould of the Barbadian Cammie Smith who, in 1960, saw Trueman and Statham go for 50 in 19 minutes. Sadly, both for himself and for our general enjoyment, Simmons could manage only 1 in the next match and later was badly injured in the match against Gloucestershire.

On the morning of the match Alan Lee, John Woodcock's successor as cricket correspondent of *The Times*, observed: 'Certainly, I have not for some years known an England selection cause such a public debate, in which the competing factors have been curiosity, hilarity, and plain outrage'. Athey, one of the two chief causes for all this, did not in the end play. Pringle, the other, did.

On a cool, cloudy morning Gatting won the toss and put West Indies in. After five overs West Indies were 32 for 0, Simmons, in particular, batting with almost indecent lack of respect. But such a brazen start against Dilley and DeFreitas was halted by some accurate, controlled bowling by Small and the despised Pringle. Simmons became over-ambitious, Greenidge was bowled by a ball of full length from Small, and Pringle had Richardson lbw. Then Richards, having made 13 off his first seven balls, was miraculously caught by Emburey, who held on to a savage slash at deep gully. At 72 for 4 West Indies were suddenly paying the price of their exuberance. Logie and Hooper, by more relaxed and sensible methods, put their side right back in the game, taking the score to 169. Both were out for 51, the innings fading away to an extent that the last six wickets fell for 48 runs. Small took 4 for 31 and Pringle, the most economical of all the five bowlers used, 1 for 26. The pitch was of the typical Edgbaston kind, slowish, slightly two-paced, and rewarding length and line rather than brute force.

A total of 217 was some 20 or 30 runs less than Richards required, and a great deal less than what was likely had he, Simmons or Greenidge lasted longer.

Gooch and Broad got off to the sort of start England wanted, fluent, assured and with few moments of anxiety. At 70 Broad left to a wonderful slip catch by Greenidge off Marshall, and at 119 Gooch, batting well within himself, to a more straightforward one by Harper off Ambrose. Lynch, sensibly sent in at a moment of comparative calm, at once set off heedlessly without taking note of Gatting's, the striker's, intentions and was run out for 0.

This sadly suicidal act was the start of some bizarre running, or rather non-running, between the wickets by Gatting and Lamb, both of whom might have been run out more than once. At 153 Lamb tried to steer an innocuous straight ball from Hooper down to third man, missed, and was bowled.

Had another wicket gone now, there is no knowing what might have happened. The light was poor, and though Gatting now and again crashed one through the covers, his timing was never quite right and he had several slices of luck.

Pringle, however, was never in trouble, taking singles off nearly every ball. The asking rate remained steady at around four an over, not an exacting task against some eccentric overs by Harper, and some mild ones from Richards and Hooper. Gatting now dominated the strike and, in no mood to be thwarted, saw England safely home with six wickets in hand, and two overs to

<table>
<tr><td colspan="2" align="center">England won the toss
WEST INDIES</td></tr>
<tr><td>C.G. Greenidge b Small</td><td>18</td></tr>
<tr><td>P.V. Simmons c Lamb b Dilley</td><td>22</td></tr>
<tr><td>R.B. Richardson lbw b Pringle</td><td>11</td></tr>
<tr><td>*I.V.A. Richards c Emburey b Small</td><td>13</td></tr>
<tr><td>A.L. Logie c Downton b Small</td><td>51</td></tr>
<tr><td>C.L. Hooper c Emburey b Small</td><td>51</td></tr>
<tr><td>†P.J.L. Dujon run out</td><td>27</td></tr>
<tr><td>R.A. Harper b Emburey</td><td>4</td></tr>
<tr><td>M.D. Marshall c Lamb b DeFreitas</td><td>6</td></tr>
<tr><td>C.E.L. Ambrose b Emburey</td><td>1</td></tr>
<tr><td>C.A. Walsh not out</td><td>2</td></tr>
<tr><td>Extras (lb 2, w 3, nb 6)</td><td>11</td></tr>
<tr><td>**Total (55 overs)**</td><td>**217**</td></tr>
</table>

Fall of wickets: 1-34, 2-50, 3-66, 4-72, 5-169, 6-180, 7-195, 8-209, 9-212
Bowling: DeFreitas 11-2-45-1; Dilley 11-0-64-1; Small 11-0-31-4; Pringle 11-5-26-1; Emburey 11-1-49-2

<table>
<tr><td colspan="2" align="center">**ENGLAND**</td></tr>
<tr><td>G.A. Gooch c Harper b Ambrose</td><td>43</td></tr>
<tr><td>B.C. Broad c Greenidge b Marshall</td><td>35</td></tr>
<tr><td>*M.W. Gatting not out</td><td>82</td></tr>
<tr><td>M.A. Lynch run out</td><td>0</td></tr>
<tr><td>A.J. Lamb b Hooper</td><td>12</td></tr>
<tr><td>D.R. Pringle not out</td><td>23</td></tr>
<tr><td>Extras (b 2, lb 9, w 7, nb 6)</td><td>24</td></tr>
<tr><td>**Total (for 4 wkts, 53 overs)**</td><td>**219**</td></tr>
</table>

P.R. Downton, J.E. Emburey, P.A.J. DeFreitas, G.C. Small, G.R. Dilley did not bat.
Fall of wickets: 1-70, 2-119, 3-121, 4-153
Bowling: Ambrose 11-1-39-1; Walsh 11-1-50-0; Marshall 11-1-32-1; Richards 7-1-29-0; Harper 7-0-33-0; Hooper 6-0-25-1
Umpires: B.J. Meyer and J. Birkenshaw
Man of the match: Gladstone Small
Result: England won by 6 wickets

spare. Small was made Man of the Match on his home ground, but it could as easily have been Gatting or Pringle.

There was, to be truthful, not all that much in it at the end. The West Indians, with little time to prepare and lacking the services of Patterson, Benjamin, and Haynes, had their chance but looked a shade rusty. It was Gatting's day, fortune favoured him, and he made the most of it. After the tribulations of the winter, it was what England badly needed, whatever might happen later.

Small (top left), having just bowled Greenidge and broken a stump, licks his lips. He took 4 for 34, had every reason to be pleased with himself and was made Man of the Match.
(Left) Emburey is displaying the evidence. Perhaps it might come in handy sometime.
(Above) The much-maligned Pringle bowled 11 overs for 26 runs and 1 wicket, that of Richardson about to be adjudged lbw.

First One-day International Edgbaston

Logie (right) *made 51, joint top score, the first of many valuable innings during the series. A calm, relaxed, yet aggressive batsman, he was the ideal kind of player to follow Richards.*

Gatting(below left) *hit his usual quota of pugnacious blows without ever quite getting on top.*

(Below, right) *It is customary at Edgbaston after these affairs for the winning batsmen to present arms on leaving the field. Pringle knows the drill, but has his bat the wrong way round.*

Second One-day International Headingley, 21 May

Bowler's day

This time Vivian Richards won the toss and put England in. The pitch was livelier than at Edgbaston, the bounce a shade uneven. At 83 for 5, with the top half of the order departed, England were in virtually the same situation as West Indies had been two days earlier, only one wicket worse off. Gooch and Broad had made 29 before Broad got an inside edge to Ambrose, and Dujon, changing direction, brought off a flying catch, the first of four. Gatting looked less confident than towards the end of his Edgbaston innings, playing and missing more in one morning than he usually does in a week. At 64 Marshall bowled him with a no-ball and then had him well caught by Richards in the gully off the next. Lynch was soon lbw and Marshall, at his most fiercesome, had taken 2 for 9 in seven overs.

Simmons now had a bowl at gentle medium pace. Lamb, swishing at a leg-side long-hop, only got a glove to it, and then Gooch, patience itself all morning and scoring a mere single per over, was out to Simmons' first ball of the afternoon.

Simmons' success and his own initial parsimony seemed to go to Richards' head, for he now bowled Simmons and himself long enough for Marshall and Ambrose to be deprived of their full quota of overs. Pringle and Downton thrived, Pringle even hitting Richards for six. Their partnership of 66, as it happened, turned the match, though it scarcely looked like doing so at the time. Bishop, tall, slim and only twenty

England, put in to bat, lost 5 wickets for 83 before Pringle and Downton added 66, mainly off Simmons and Richards. Gatting (above) was bowled by Marshall off a no-ball and caught in the gully off the next. The bowlers beat the bat more often than they hit it, something that was as true at the end of the match as it was at the start.

West Indies won the toss
ENGLAND
G.A. Gooch c Greenidge b Simmons	32
B.C. Broad c Dujon b Ambrose	13
*M.W. Gatting c Richards b Marshall	18
M.A. Lynch lbw b Marshall	2
A.J. Lamb c Dujon b Simmons	2
D.R. Pringle c Dujon b Walsh	39
†P.R. Downton c Dujon b Bishop	30
J.E. Emburey c Ambrose b Bishop	8
P.A.J. DeFreitas not out	15
G.C. Small not out	7
Extras (b 3, lb 1, w 3, nb 13)	20
Total (for 8 wkts, 55 overs)	**186**

G.R. Dilley did not bat
Fall of wickets: 1-29, 2-64, 3-72, 4-80, 5-83, 6-149, 7-154, 8-169
Bowling: Walsh 11-0-39-1; Ambrose 7-2-19-1; Marshall 9-1-29-2; Bishop 11-1-32-2; Simmons 9-2-30-2; Richards 8-0-33-0

WEST INDIES
C.G. Greenidge c Downton b Small	21
P.V. Simmons b DeFreitas	1
R.B. Richardson c Downton b Dilley	1
*I.V.A. Richards b Small	31
A.L. Logie c Lynch b Dilley	8
C.L. Hooper lbw b Pringle	12
†P.J.L. Dujon b Pringle	12
M.D. Marshall c Downton b Gooch	1
C.E.L. Ambrose c Downton b Pringle	23
C.A. Walsh b Emburey	18
I.R. Bishop not out	2
Extras (lb 3, w 3, nb 3)	9
Total (46.3 overs)	**139**

Fall of wickets: 1-2, 2-11, 3-38, 4-67, 5-67, 6-83, 7-84, 8-104, 9-132
Bowling: Dilley 11-0-45-2; DeFreitas 9-2-29-1; Small 9-2-11-2; Pringle 11-0-30-3; Gooch 3-0-12-1; Emburey 3.3-0-9-1
Umpires: D.J. Constant and D.R. Shepherd
Man of the match: D.R. Pringle
Result: England won by 47 runs

Second One-day International Headingley

Pringle (right) had another fine match, making 39 and taking 3 for 30. He bowled a full length and straight, getting the occasional one to cut back or move away. He looks splendidly aggressive here, but generally his demeanour – mouth open like a fledgling waiting for food, shoulders slumped, gait heavy – suggests dreamy fatalism rather than animation.

years old, bowled a full stint of eleven overs to take 2 for 32 and impress everyone in the process with his pace off the pitch and movement off the seam.

West Indies, needing only 187 to win, made a disastrous start. DeFreitas bowled Simmons at 2 and, at 11, Dilley had Richardson caught at the wicket. With Greenidge and Richards together, the match was now crucially balanced. There were, though, none of the early fireworks from Richards as at Edgbaston, the dogged example of Gooch suggesting a more profitable way home. Both got on to the front foot as often as they could and the runs, off hostile and accurate bowling by DeFreitas and Small, came mostly off forward pushes. At 38, however, Greenidge got an edge to an intended slash at Small and then Richards, having made 31 with rare concern yet with six boundaries, dragged a widish ball on to his stumps.

With Hooper and Dujon still in, the West Indies had batsmen enough left and overs to

spare. But Pringle, keeping the ball well up, removed them both, Dujon in particular being bowled by a beauty. Gooch was brought on for three overs, enough for him to get Marshall to touch an outswinger.

Ambrose and Walsh, with the innings apparently in ruins, now decided to spin the match out as long as possible. For every time they made contact they probably missed three times, mainly against Pringle and DeFreitas. Walsh was badly missed at slip by Gatting off DeFreitas and the score began to tick up, 104 for 8 reaching 132. Pringle eventually found the elusive edge of Ambrose's bat and Emburey, brought on for the first time, yorked Walsh.

The winning margin of 47 runs was considerable in such a low-scoring match in which four batsmen reached 30 but none 40. It had been a bowlers' day, the faster bowlers on both sides making life uncomfortable for each batsman in turn. There were few boundaries and, apart from Pringle's six, scarcely any big hits.

Gatting (far left) realises he has forgotten his Financial Times and missed an easy one in the slips – no great consequence at the time it seemed although Walsh (left), the beneficiary, and Ambrose took the score from 104 for 8 to 132 before Pringle parted them. Walsh was then bowled by Emburey, allowed only three overs.

Instead of arms being presented at the end of the match as at Edgbaston, Headingley brings on dancing girls, the local racial mix being symbolised by the black and white uniform and stockings. The police are formally offered libations they are obliged to accept.

England's series

The result might have been of academic interest but there was still every incentive for Gatting, before a full house, to show his home crowd what England had been up to. It was a rotten sort of day, at least until early evening, and there were five breaks in play, either for rain or bad light. By the end of it West Indies, put in to bat, had managed no more than 125 for 6, with only five overs in hand. It was difficult to remember more concertedly accurate bowling by any England side in this form of cricket and the fielding, achieving three run-outs, was without blemish.

The morning produced only one ball before the players went off, but when they returned at two o'clock it was plain that batting would be a struggle. The ball was moving all over the place and though the bounce was fairer than at either Edgbaston or Headingley it was only the experience and technical skills of Greenidge and Haynes that kept England out for seventeen overs.

Once the opening partnership of 40 was broken, a slick pick-up and throw by Broad to the bowler's end running out Haynes, wickets began to fall at regular intervals. Greenidge, having hit Pringle's first two balls for 4 and 6, was superbly caught at deep square-leg off Emburey by DeFreitas. Richardson touched a good one from Pringle, once again finding admirable length and line after his unnerving start, and at 80 Logie, answering Richards' call for a single to cover, was smartly thrown out by Lamb.

Anything like a considerable total now seemed to depend on Richards. But, chewing as relentlessly as ever, he was never able to dominate as he likes. It was no great surprise when, trying to force DeFreitas off the back foot, he was for the second time in three innings caught by Emburey in the gully.

The sun came out at half-past six and Hooper, going for a second run to long leg, was well beaten by DeFreitas's racing pick-up and flat throw. Small had bowled as well as in the previous two matches and Radford, replacing Dilley, had bustled in to good effect. DeFreitas, who had started with five maidens in a row, had one of those days cricketers dream about: Richards' wicket, a brilliant catch, and a long throw to the top of the stumps that left the batsman drowning.

Next morning, with five overs to go, Marshall and Dujon threw caution to the winds. They might have been content with 30 runs, instead they got 53 (Marshall hit two sixes and three fours) and only lost a wicket off the very last ball. A contest had, after all, been arranged.

For a couple of hours, against fine bowling by Walsh and Marshall, Gooch and Broad grazed, anxious perhaps to give the modest crowd as much play as possible for their money. Walsh, in improved batting conditions, bowled 8 overs for 6 runs and struck Gooch on the side of the head in the process. The over rate was as slow as the

England won the toss

WEST INDIES

C.G. Greenidge c DeFreitas b Emburey		39
D.L. Haynes run out		10
R.B. Richardson c Downton b Pringle		13
*I.V.A. Richards c Emburey b DeFreitas		9
A.L. Logie run out		0
C.L. Hooper run out		12
†P.J.L. Dujon not out		30
M.D. Marshall b Emburey		41
Extras (b 2, lb 10, w 12)		24
Total (7 wkts, 55 overs)		**178**

W.K.M. Benjamin, C.A. Walsh, I.R. Bishop did not bat.
Fall of wickets: 1-40, 2-75, 3-79, 4-79, 5-95, 6-111, 7-178
Bowling: DeFreitas 11-5-20-1; Radford 11-2-29-0; Small 10-1-34-0; Pringle 11-4-27-1; Emburey 10-1-53-2; Gooch 2-1-3-0

ENGLAND

G.A. Gooch st Dujon b Hooper		28
B.C. Broad b Bishop		34
*M.W. Gatting not out		40
M.A. Lynch b Bishop		6
A.J. Lamb not out		30
Extras (b 6, lb 17, w 5, nb 14)		42
Total (3 wkts, 50 overs)		**180**

D.R. Pringle, †P.R. Downton, J.E. Emburey, P.A.J. DeFreitas, G.C. Small, N.V. Radford did not bat.
Fall of wickets: 1-71, 2-108, 3-124
Bowling: Marshall 9-2-21-0; Walsh 11-5-11-0; Bishop 11-1-33-2; Benjamin 9-0-38-0; Hooper 10-0-54-1
Umpires: H.D. Bird and N.T. Plews
Man of the match: P.A.J. DeFreitas
Men of the series: M.W. Gatting (England) and M.D. Marshall (West Indies)
Result: England won by 7 wickets
England won series 3-0

batting, 12 overs for 13 runs in the first hour, 13 overs for 30 runs in the second. The 50 came up in the twenty-seventh over, a third of these runs being extras.

Having established the innings with proper thoughtfulness and seen the asking rate rise from just above three runs per over to nearly five, Gooch became comparatively skittish. He was soon out, however, stumped off Hooper as he backed away to cut.

Gatting's arrival speeded things up considerably. He hammered Hooper high over mid-off and then through the covers in his first over and never looked back. Broad lost his off stump to Bishop, bowling with high arm and loose, breasting approach, and soon after it was Lynch's middle stump that did cartwheels. Lynch's curious stance, almost back on his wicket and with little detectable movement forward or back, did his cause no good against a bowler whipping the ball down the hill at him.

With ten overs left England needed 44. Lamb immediately hit Benjamin and Bishop smartly back over their heads. What had begun at a snail's pace ended at a gallop. Five of the ten overs were not needed and England lost no more wickets.

All in all, the three one-day matches had been both an eye-opener and, from England's point of view, a comfort. But they were not the real thing and no-one believed that they were.

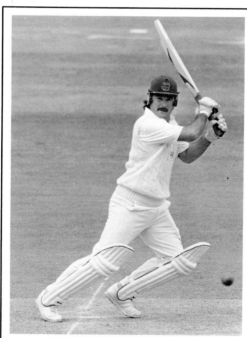

(Above) *England's funeral march to victory was speeded up by the arrival of Lamb, who started hitting the fast bowlers back over their heads, somewhat to their surprise.*

(Above) *Haynes, just settling in, is run out at the bowler's end by an unusually sharp piece of fielding by Broad. From 40 for 0 West Indies declined to 111 for 6, three of the wickets falling to run-outs. Dickie Bird, in his 100th Test, looks delighted at the prospect of raising his finger.*
(Below) *Richards congratulates Gatting on the 'whitewash'. He knows his players, having just run themselves out, are also running themselves in.*

Fine start, but clouds

There was no shortage of rain at Trent Bridge and Courtney Walsh (above), for whom the umpire usually carries an umbrella, has to make his own cover. Small children on the boundary fled, thinking they had seen a bogey man. Walsh took no wickets but deserved several, his 20 overs costing a mere 39 runs.

England's efficient and professional dispatch of West Indies in the three one-day matches was a boost to morale but no guarantee of further success. By mid-afternoon of the first day here any lingering fears were beginning to slink away. Gatting had won a good toss and on a fairly passive pitch Gooch and Broad were cruising contentedly past the hundred. Then clouds began to build up and Marshall, reducing pace, suddenly swung the ball disconcertingly. Whereas batting before lunch had been a pleasure it now became a question of survival. Gooch was dropped at slip off Marshall, beaten by him several times in one over, and then bowled. The ball swung hugely from off to leg and Gooch, launching himself into a cover drive, dragged it into his stumps. Gatting lasted for only fifteen balls before fending a shortish ball to Logie, freshly summoned up to short-leg.

Broad now found runs increasingly hard to come by and he was stagnant when, in the last over before tea, Marshall bowled him off the inside edge, Broad neither quite forward nor back. The last ball of that over was another inswinger and Lamb was lbw. So 125 for 0 had become 161 for 4.

Gower, without ever looking on good terms with himself, jogged along for an hour and a half, but he was lucky to be dropped at slip off Ambrose, Greenidge's second spill of the day. Far from disciplining himself as a result he played a dreadful, firm-footed swish one over later and was caught at the wicket. No further disasters followed, Pringle and Downton adding 34 and taking England to 220 for 5. It had been Marshall's day, his 24 overs for four wickets and 54 runs a masterly and varied demonstration of the bowler's art.

England might still have hoped for another hundred runs. In the event they managed only a further 25. Marshall beat Pringle with an inswinger of full length before he had got his eyes open and then, going round the wicket, removed Emburey. Ambrose announced himself with two bouncers at Jarvis, but thereafter pitched the ball up, hitting the stumps of DeFreitas, Jarvis and Dilley in turn. Each departed as if nothing was to be gained by hanging around.

The light was now generally murky, turning to heavy rain in the afternoon before clearing. Greenidge and Haynes found they had to work for their runs, not least because so many balls, especially from DeFreitas, were wide of the stumps. It took just under two hours for the 50 to go up, at which point Jarvis got one to lift off a length to Greenidge, only for Emburey at first slip to move late to an ankle-high catch. Greenidge, like Gower the day before, seemed determined to compensate the bowler, slashing at a shorter ball in the same over and edging it to Downton. Emburey's relief was noticeably evident.

With time left for only half a dozen overs Gatting brought on Emburey who has had some success against Richardson. He got his sixth ball to bounce and turn and Gatting took a good, one-handed catch at short-leg. Any notions that conditions might now favour spin or that speed in the fading light could do further damage were quickly dismissed by Richards. He received only twenty-three balls and he hit five of them to the boundary, almost with an air of amusement. Pringle bowled seven overs for four runs but, after Marshall, England's bowlers looked mostly on the tame side.

Saturday was almost a wash-out, its melancholy relieved by an innings of savage glamour by Richards and one of classical correctness by Hooper. There were numerous interruptions for bad light and drizzle, and rapidly though they progressed West Indies were only able to add another 158 runs, for the loss of Haynes and Richards. Haynes got a nasty one from Jarvis, Downton diving to catch him off his glove; and Richards, first ball after yet another break, drove at DeFreitas, the ball hurtling towards the throat of Gooch at second slip. Mercifully Gooch got his hands there, and though knocked flat on his back by the force of it, held on. Richards hit twelve fours and a six, beginning with swirling shots over and through the covers off Dilley and Jarvis, and ending with vast and demoralising blows off Emburey (seven overs for 62).

Over the weekend the weather cheered up, and England's chances of saving the match, despite the loss of over a day's play already, seemed dependent on dealing in comparable style with the West Indies tail. This they did not succeed in doing: Logie and Dujon went comparatively quietly and Hooper seemingly set cool for a stylish

gather

hundred, fell foul of one of DeFreitas' better deliveries, but the worst was ahead. Emburey was given another turn, and Marshall set about him as greedily as Richards had done. Ambrose, for the first hour scarcely lifting his bat, tucked in with a six of his own, and together these two frolicked nearly another hundred runs. England's fielding deteriorated, and Gatting seemed to have his mind on other things.

So, 203 behind, Gooch and Broad began on the undramatic task of survival. Broad lasted eighty minutes, never really happy with the bounce and taking several blows before almost resignedly following a slanting delivery from Ambrose. No more wickets fell that evening, Gooch, often troubled by Walsh's late movement off the pitch, finishing with 38 and Gatting 8.

When play began on the last morning it was still hard, on the basis of their first innings, so see England keeping the West Indies bowlers at bay long enough. In fact, steered to safety by a dignified and dogged 146 by Gooch, they lost only two more wickets. Gatting, after adding 77 with Gooch, had his off stump sent cartwheeling by a vintage leg-cutter, though at half pace, from Marshall; and Gooch, late in the day and with honour salvaged, got a beauty from Patterson. Marshall was absent after lunch with a recurrence of a rib injury but Gooch had made plain that he meant to stay. He was beaten from time to time by balls darting in at him or cutting away but his timing grew sweeter and his manner lordlier. Gower was some time finding his touch but by the end he, too, leaning the ball through the covers in the old way, finished up somewhere near his real form. There was always just enough in the pitch to suggest that any one ball could change the match brutally, but such edges as there were never quite went to hand or were put down. West Indies bowled decently but on a sunny afternoon the batsmen had their measure.

About the pitch Jackie Hendriks, the West Indies manager, commented: 'It's not the surface I thought we would have seen at Trent Bridge. It is difficult to play shots. Test cricket should be played with consistent pace and bounce'. This, of course, was said before Richards' innings and, later on, those of Hooper and Marshall.

England won the toss
ENGLAND
First Innings

G.A. Gooch b Marshall	73
B.C. Broad b Marshall	54
*M.W. Gatting c Logie b Marshall	5
D.I. Gower c Dujon b Ambrose	18
A.J. Lamb lbw b Marshall	0
D.R. Pringle b Marshall	39
†P.R. Downton not out	16
J.E. Emburey c Dujon b Marshall	0
P.A.J. DeFreitas b Ambrose	3
P. Jarvis b Ambrose	6
G.R. Dilley b Ambrose	2
Extras (lb 13, w 5, nb 11)	29
Total	**245**

Fall of wickets: 1-125, 2-141, 3-161, 4-161, 5-186, 6-223, 7-223, 8-235, 9-243
Bowling: Marshall 30-4-69-6; Patterson 16-2-49-0; Ambrose 26-10-53-4; Walsh 20-4-39-0; Hooper 8-1-20-0; Richards 1-0-2-0

WEST INDIES
First Innings

C.G. Greenidge c Downton b Jarvis	25
D.L. Haynes c Downton b Jarvis	60
R.B. Richardson c Gatting b Emburey	17
*I.V.A. Richards c Gooch b DeFreitas	80
C.L. Hooper c Downton b DeFreitas	84
A.L. Logie c Gooch b Pringle	20
†P.J.L. Dujon c and b Dilley	16
M.D. Marshall b Emburey	72
C.E.L. Ambrose run out	43
C.A. Walsh not out	3
Extras (b 6, lb 8, nb 14)	28
Total (9 wkts dec)	**448**

B.P. Patterson did not bat.
Fall of wickets: 1-54, 2-84, 3-159, 4-231, 5-271, 6-309, 7-334, 8-425, 9-448
Bowling: Dilley 34-5-101-1; DeFreitas 27-5-93-2; Jarvis 18.1-1-63-2; Pringle 34-11-82-1; Emburey 16-4-95-2

ENGLAND
Second Innings

G.A. Gooch c Dujon b Patterson	146
B.C. Broad c Dujon b Ambrose	16
*M.W. Gatting b Marshall	29
D.I. Gower not out	88
A.J. Lamb not out	6
Extras (lb 10, nb 6)	16
Total (for 3 wkts)	**301**

Fall of wickets: 1-39, 2-116, 3-277
Bowling: Marshall 13-4-23-1; Patterson 24-6-69-1; Ambrose 23-4-56-1; Walsh 25-5-84-0; Richards 9-1-26-0; Hooper 14-1-33-0
Umpires: J. Birkenshaw and H.D. Bird
Man of the match: M.D. Marshall
Result: Match Drawn

Gatting, lasting only for fifteen balls, had no chance to improve his sun tan. Instead (above) he basked at the dressing-room window in his last bit of good weather for some time.

The best batting on a rain-ravaged Saturday came from Richards and Hooper. Richards scored 80 rather scornfully, mainly at the expense of Dilley, Jarvis and Emburey. Hooper, patient, correct, and always pleasing to watch, made 84.

First Test
Trent Bridge

Gooch (right) had enjoyed his batting on the first morning, but in the afternoon clouds built up, Marshall reduced his pace, and the ball began to swing disconcertingly. Here Gooch, having been beaten several times in a row by Marshall, as well as dropped off him at slip, finds himself bowled off the inside edge, having launched himself into an off-drive.

Broad (below) is comprehensively bowled by Patterson, but it was a no-ball. Marshall later bowled him in the last over before tea, Broad, comparatively sprightly early on, having virtually seized up.

Broad is usually associated with knocking stumps over rather than knocking them in. However, since this was Patterson's no-ball, there was no need for umbrage. Patterson though, (below) took a less rosy view of the matter, convinced apparently that decapitation was the only answer.

First Test
Trent Bridge

Pringle (right) does not often endanger close fielders but Richardson has either seen a snake or chosen levitation in preference to emasculation.

(Below) Few days have been more interrupted by rain than the third day of this match. Umpire Bird probably enjoyed himself and, while Birkenshaw got a damp pate, his own hair achieved a becoming gloss.

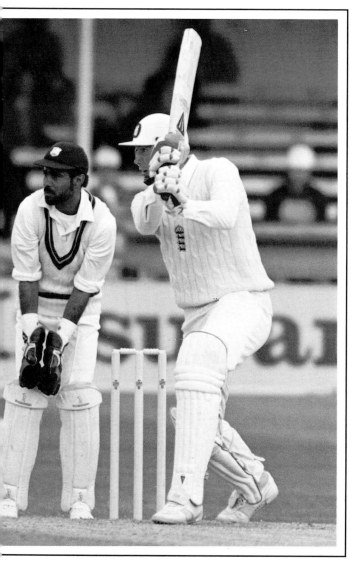

Bird grimaces (above) *as if Ambrose might easily elbow him in the eye. After a spate of bouncers at the tail-enders, Ambrose decided to concentrate on yorkers, like his equally tall and gangling great predecessor Garner. He hit the stumps of DeFreitas, Jarvis and Dilley in quick succession and finished with 4 for 53.*

As West Indies leave the field (left) Richards demonstrates to Walsh, Dujon, Ambrose and Richardson the size of the one that got away.

21

First Test
Trent Bridge

Richardson, often out to Emburey in the Caribbean, is well caught by Gatting – muzzled and told not to talk to the press – at short-leg. This ball from Emburey bounced and turned, seeming to suggest possibilities for the off-spinner. They proved to be whether Richards or Marshall would hit him for 4 or 6.

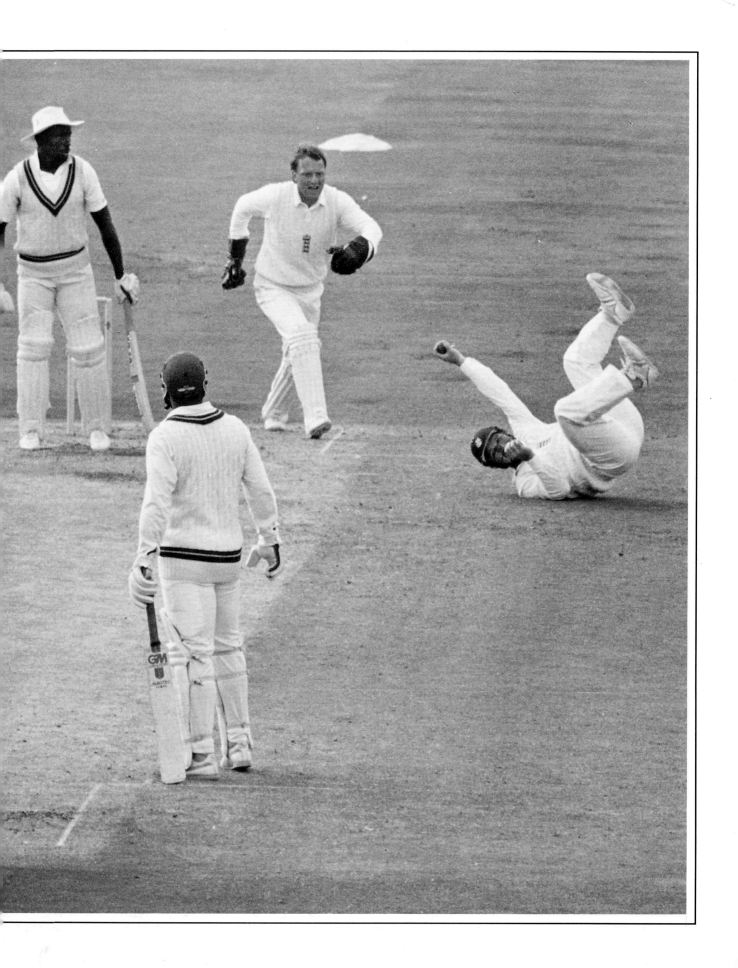

First Test
Trent Bridge

Richards (below) *who rarely bothers to play himself in these days, hits Emburey for an immense six. Downton seems fearful for the spectators' safety or he may have spotted a converging aircraft.*

Hooper, who looks certain to succeed Richards as the West Indian batsman of the 1990s, drives Emburey with free swing of the bat. He played spin and pace with equal assurance.

First Test
Trent Bridge

(Right) *Marshall, finding his helmet oppressive in Nottinghamshire's tropical climate, signals for his floppy hat. Ambrose seems to think it a bit of a joke, but then he does not often get the chance to share in a stand of 91 and hit sixes himself.*

(Below) *The head of an Emperor. Richards likes to keep in radio communication with his troops at all times.*

Marshall (left), having taken 6 for 69, made 72 runs, most of them correctly but some with lavish abandon. Emburey's 16 overs cost him 95 runs and, had circumstances not changed so drastically, must have endangered his Test place.

This hit by Ambrose appears to have gone a long way and Emburey at slip looks almost delighted that for once it was not off him. As a batsman Ambrose has no half-measures; either he pushes out like a timid rabbit or swings mightily.

First Test
Trent Bridge

Ambrose was determined to get Broad out one way or another. In fact he soon had him caught at the wicket, rather wearily following a ball slanted across him.

(Above) *Patterson, with 1 for 118 in the match, was the least impressive of the West Indian bowlers. However, despite Umpire Birkenshaw's suspicious peering, he shows the regulation ten studs to the batsman.*

(Left) *Gooch, with 73 and 146, saved the match for England. He was, like everyone else in the conditions, beaten from time to time but his concentration was absolute and by the end his manner quite lordly.*

First Test
Trent Bridge

(Below) *With the pace at which the West Indians bowl, any straying in direction makes Dujon leap about more than any goalkeeper. This ball has passed Gower outside the off stump and ended up far to Dujon's right.*

Everything is right about Gatting's stroke (opposite), except that his off stump has gone flying. Marshall, having revived an old rib injury, was bowling a little over half-pace but this was a beauty.

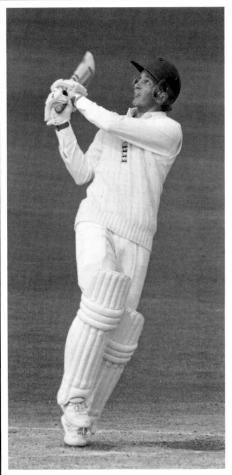

A fetching glimpse of the remembered Gower (left). It was some time before it came, but in the end he was moving into line and timing the ball with the old sweetness.

(Below) Sometimes pictures really do tell a story. Gower looks fearfully towards his captain, storm clouds ahead, meteorological and otherwise.

NOTE ON THE PHOTOGRAPHS

The section of colour photographs which follows is an album of the 1988 Test series. Rather than repeat the chronological arrangement which is the form of the rest of the book, the pictures have been chosen deliberately to give an overall impression of the different events and personalities, and climate, of the whole summer.

All the photographs in the book were taken with Nikon cameras and lenses. The cameras used for the action photographs were Nikon F3's and the lenses were 600mm f/4, 500mm f/4 and 300mm f/4.5. The black and white photographs were all taken on Ilford XP1 film, and the colour photographs, in the section which follows, were taken on Fujichrome 100, Kodachrome 64 and 200.

All the black and white prints were made on Ilford Multigrade paper by my long-suffering and ever-cheerful assistant Jan Traylen.

Yes, one does watch every ball; but no, one doesn't photograph every ball. The 150-odd black and white photographs in this book are distilled from some 5000 exposures taken during the 1988 summer. Some of the photographs are taken by remote control – you might like to guess which? (There is a clue in the series of Chris Broad and Patterson's no-ball on pages 18 and 19).

Patrick Eagar

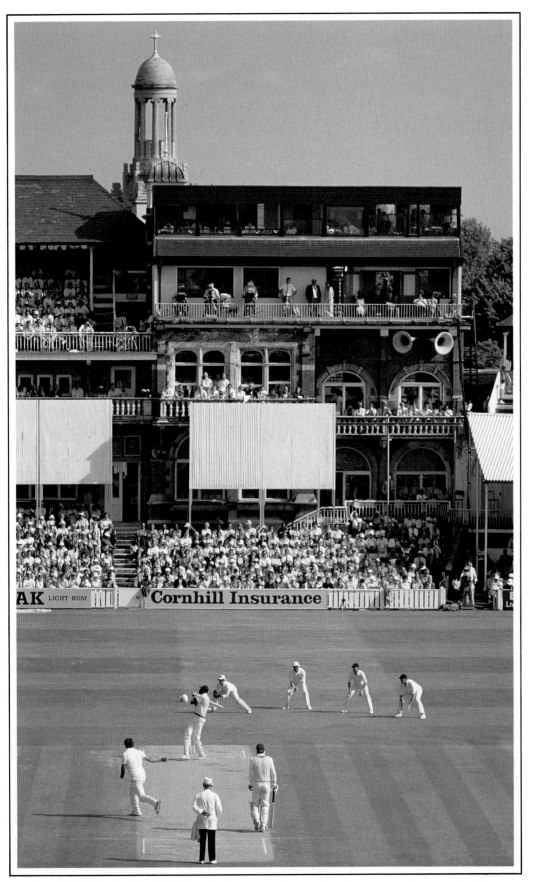

At The Oval Curtley Ambrose hits out. As a batsman he has two speeds: dead slow or flat out. He liked to tease the bowler by looking a complete novice and then hit him out of sight.

(Opposite) *Gower at Trent Bridge seems more anxious about his hair than his helmet, though unless he's wearing a wig the helmet could do more damage.*

Richards looks as if he might have missed a vocation as Regimental Sergeant-Major – at least as far as voice, if not turn-out is concerned.

Ambrose, loose, high-stepping, and his arm clearing the sight-screen, was never collared. From his height and on his length runs were rare commodities.

Dickie Bird may look as if he is lifting his skirts preliminary to a paddle at Brighton, but Dilley is focused on the far end. Fit, he was formidable; less than fit, banal.

(Opposite above) *Long-leg, and the only thing longer than Ambrose is his own shadow. You'd think he'd need binoculars to see what was going on.*

(Opposite below) *A photographer's life is not always a happy one; sometimes more like manning a gun in the North Sea.*

Viv Richards is caught at Old Trafford; but, unfortunately for Emburey, the bowler, by some bright spark in the stand behind him.

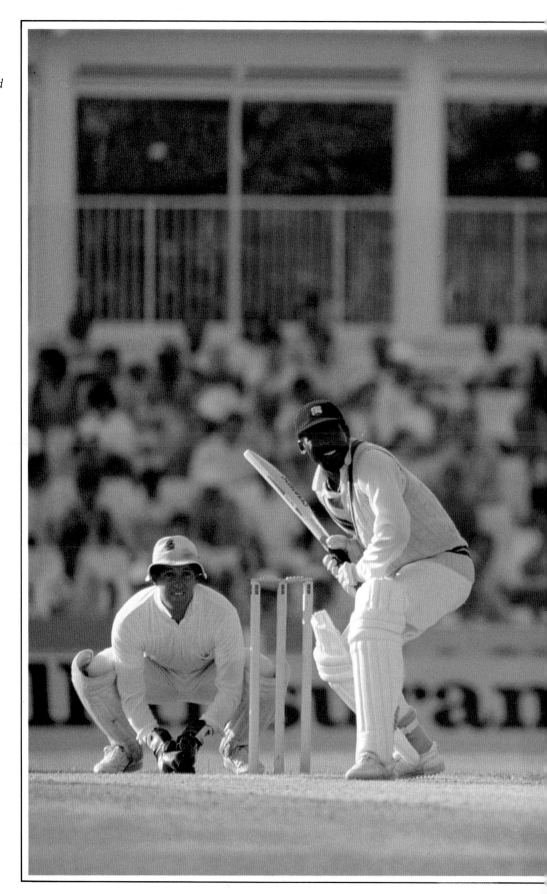

Greenidge, facing Childs at The Oval, is all compressed power. Any second he will spring like a tiger, or simply bide his time, bat straight, head to handle.

(Right) *Lamb does not usually wear his helmet on the back of his head, but Patterson put the breeze up him now and again, as here at Lord's. Patterson was possibly the fastest of the West Indies' bowlers but the least suited to games of attrition.*

(Below) *Robin Smith seemed sometimes to have to play round his legs, the front pad in the way, as here against Harper at The Oval. But he keeps his head still, watches the ball, and, when he can, cuts with a woodcutter's swing of the axe.*

(Opposite) *The feet have moved, the bat swung freely. There were a dozen or so glimpses of the golden beauty of Gower's batting, but they became fewer and fewer, the fallibility more blatant.*

(Right) *Greenidge looks hungry, for runs and cake equally. He was prone to a variety of ailments, but usually came good when necessary.*

(Opposite) *Capel has bowled Richards at Old Trafford, so the scorebook says. But in truth the great man, not for the first time during the summer, has got himself out, dragging a widish ball on to his stumps.*

(Opposite above) *The pavilion at Old Trafford may not possess quite the grandeur of Lord's, but with its domes and hanging baskets of flowers it's the next best thing. What's more it's seen a thing or two.*

(Opposite below) *Not fishermen hauling in their nets, nor sailors trying to right a catamaran, but the long-suffering Old Trafford ground staff during a sudden downpour.*

(Left) *Ambrose exercising, at the same time rehearsing for the knobbly-knees competition. Predictable comparisons with Joel Garner did him no harm. He could contain, he could bounce, and he learned to york.*

Gatting loses captaincy

During the weekend of the Trent Bridge Test match Mike Gatting celebrated his birthday, his thirty-first. After a convivial and lengthy evening at the Red Lion Inn, Rothley, near Leicester, the England captain invited a barmaid, Louise Shipman, to his hotel room, where they were alone together. These facts emerged when the story was subsequently splashed over the pages of the *Sun*, *Today* and the *Daily Mirror*, among other tabloid newspapers. Gatting, under questioning, agreed that he and Miss Shipman had been alone together, but that no impropriety had taken place. On the other hand the barmaid alleged to reporters that Gatting had laid her over his four-poster bed and that there had been sexual intercourse. She later expressed regret at the outcome of her disclosures. One of Louise Shipman's colleagues behind the bar was even more forthcoming, asserting that the two of them kept scores of their sexual activities, the numbers in recent weeks reaching figures that would be welcomed by most English batsmen. Other Test players were alleged to have been among the weekend celebrants.

Peter May, the chairman of the selectors, announced to a packed Press conference that though they had accepted the captain's version of events, 'his irresponsible behaviour' had made it necessary for his invitation to lead England at Lord's to be withdrawn.

Gatting said that his solicitors would be issuing writs for libel against the newspapers concerned.

There was a certain lack of logic about all this and Gatting received as much public sympathy about his sacking as he did censure. It was felt that, in the circumstances, he would not be in the right frame of mind to play in the second Test at Lord's and he asked not to be considered. Instead, he made three centuries for Middlesex during the next ten days, during which an account of his Faisalabad slanging match with the Pakistani umpire, Shakoor Rana, appeared in the *Sunday Times*. It was an extract from his autobiography *Leading from the Front*, this particular chapter being credited and copyrighted to his co-writer Angela Patmore.

WEEK IN REVIEW: OPINION

Goodbye to Mr Gatting

THE SUNDAY TIMES 12 JUNE 1988

THE SUNDAY TIMES

THERE WAS a time when it was every small English boy's ambition to be captain of England. Not at football, but at cricket. Cricket was a game of fair play. To be the cricket captain of England was to hold the paramount position of any male athlete in the realm.

It is a position of supreme responsibility. The captain is the leader on and off the field. He is the master strategist. He co-selects the team. And because cricket has a special place in (not British) cult...

TODAY Friday June 10 1988

Today
JUNE 10 1988

Oh Lord's, what a team

WHAT a bunch of hypocritical thick-heads the English Test selectors are.

On the one hand, they sack Gatting for taking a girl to his bedchamber in the middle of the night. On the other hand, they affirm their belief that the maiden, if we can describe her as such, was not bowled over by Gatting, or anything else of an untoward nature took place.

Why then sack him? These guardians of morality would, of course, argue that Gatting was guilty of a cardinal sin if he was not tucked up with a good Wisden (its only scores are cricket) by 10.30 each night.

At best, the silly asses at Lord's are like a bunch of immature prefects grandly parading their authority in a sixth-form common room at a public school.

ENGLAND SKIPPER ON THE WAY OUT

SHAMED
Sex scandal costs Gatting captaincy

Daily Mirror

MIKE GATTING AND THE BARMAID
Waitress tells of sex romps with Test captain

Cricket in crisis as Lord's call for probe

Gatting's drink and sex shame

A real chance wasted

Moxon replaced Gatting, Small took over from DeFreitas. Emburey, Gatting's vice-captain on the last two overseas tours, was preferred as captain initially for this one match to Gooch, Gower, or Kim Barnett, the Derbyshire captain, an outsider highly respected among the counties and in fine form. On the morning of the match Simon Barnes in *The Times* contrasted Gatting's misdemeanour to that of Emburey and Gooch, the new captain and vice-captain, who had 'sold English cricket down the river' by taking part in a rebel tour to South Africa. About Gatting, Alan Lee, *The Times* cricket correspondent wrote, 'In the past few months Gatting's reaction to criticism has often been mulish, sometimes rude . . . He came into the job carrying widespread media goodwill but, to some extent, he has surrendered this, which was sad for us and unhelpful for him . . . There will be no smugness at his fall from grace, no jealous chuckling, only a sense of sadness that one whose life has been wrapped up in cricket should have failed in a job he had never dreamed he could aspire to'. Whatever views people held about the rightness or wrongness of Gatting's sacking, what was indisputable was that authority had bowed to the gutter press.

On a warm, sunny morning Richards won the toss and after some thought decided to bat. Richie Benaud on TV described the pitch as 'a belter', worth at least 400 runs. However, no sooner had play begun than a dank mist, under steadily increasing cloud, spread over North London. 21-0 became 54-5, a scarcely credible transformation initiated by some magnificently sustained outswing bowling from the Nursery End by Dilley. Haynes was brilliantly taken by Moxon at short-leg, Greenidge fell to a diving catch by Downton, Richardson was neatly picked up at second slip, and, most crucial of all, Richards went to another catch behind the wicket. Meanwhile, Hooper had fallen at the other end to Small.

Shirt-sleeve weather, and Greenidge and Haynes look forward to a sunny start. But within minutes clouds rolled up and 21 for 0 became 54 for 5.

The afternoon belonged to Logie and Dujon. Both were dropped but, batting with style and spirit, they added 130 before Emburey had Dujon playing on to the last ball before tea.

Afterwards, the last four wickets were polished off for only 25 runs, Logie slashing Small to cover and the bowlers batting as if not having counted on being called upon.

England at close of play were 20 for 1, Broad having been rapidly disposed of by Marshall. Next morning England reached 112 for 2, with Gooch taking root and Gower alternately delighting and riding his luck. It was again cool and overcast but there was reason to suppose England might end the day with runs and wickets in hand. At 129, however, Gower hooked Walsh to square-leg and Marshall, after an early spell

of only four overs, returned. Gooch, his scoring stokes having virtually dried up, was immediately beaten by an outswinger and then bowled next ball by one that flicked in between bat and pad. Lamb was lbw to another that cut back and also kept low, Downton went in similar fashion, Jarvis mis-hit a slower ball, and Dilley lost his off stump first ball. The last eight wickets had fallen for 53. England, after the high hopes of the morning, were all out for 165, 44 runs behind, and Marshall finished with 6 for 32 in 18 overs. He had improved on all that Dilley had done the day before, mainly because of his greater variety and his ability to cut the ball back as well as move it away.

It was impossible not to feel that England had wasted a real chance and that West Indies, whatever the conditions, would now steadily tighten their grip.

So it proved. On Saturday the sun came out and Greenidge cut and drove his way to a hundred. Richards, establishing himself with a six off Emburey, sauntered to 72 before dragging Pringle on to his stumps. Then, for the second time in the match, Logie and Dujon put the batting strengths of

West Indies won the toss
WEST INDIES
First Innings

C.G. Greenidge c Downton b Dilley	22
D.L. Haynes c Moxon b Dilley	12
R.B. Richardson c Emburey b Dilley	5
*I.V.A. Richards c Downton b Dilley	6
C.L. Hooper c Downton b Small	3
A.L. Logie c Emburey b Small	81
†P.J.L. Dujon b Emburey	53
M.D. Marshall c Gooch b Dilley	11
C.E.L. Ambrose c Gower b Small	0
C.A. Walsh not out	9
B.P. Patterson b Small	0
Extras (lb 6, nb 1)	7
Total	**209**

Fall of wickets: 1-21, 2-40, 3-47, 4-50, 5-54, 6-184, 7-199, 8-199, 9-199

Bowling: Dilley 23-6-55-5; Jarvis 13-2-47-0; Small 18.5-5-64-4; Pringle 7-3-20-0; Emburey 6-2-17-1

WEST INDIES
Second Innings

C.G. Greenidge c Emburey b Dilley	103
D.L. Haynes c Downton b Dilley	5
R.B. Richardson lbw b Pringle	26
*I.V.A. Richards b Pringle	72
C.L. Hooper c Downton b Jarvis	11
A.L. Logie not out	95
†P.J.L. Dujon b Jarvis	52
M.D. Marshall b Jarvis	6
C.E.L. Ambrose b Dilley	0
C.A. Walsh b Dilley	0
B.P. Patterson c Downton b Jarvis	2
Extras (lb 19, w 1, nb 5)	25
Total	**397**

Fall of wickets: 1-32, 2-115, 3-198, 4-226, 5-240, 6-371, 7-379, 8-380, 9-384

Bowling: Dilley 27-6-73-4; Small 19-1-76-0; Jarvis 26-3-107-4; Emburey 15-1-62-0; Pringle 21-4-60-2

ENGLAND
First Innings

G.A. Gooch b Marshall	44
B.C. Broad lbw b Marshall	0
M.D. Moxon c Richards b Ambrose	26
D.I. Gower c sub b Walsh	46
A.J. Lamb lbw b Marshall	10
D.R. Pringle c Dujon b Walsh	1
†P.R. Downton lbw b Marshall	11
*J.E. Emburey b Patterson	7
G.C. Small not out	5
P.W. Jarvis c Haynes b Marshall	7
G.R. Dilley b Marshall	0
Extras (lb 6, nb 2)	8
Total	**165**

Fall of wickets: 1-13, 2-58, 3-112, 4-129, 5-134, 6-140, 7-153, 8-157, 9-165

Bowling: Marshall 18-5-32-6; Patterson 13-3-52-1; Ambrose 12-1-39-1; Walsh 16-6-36-2

ENGLAND
Second Innings

G.A. Gooch lbw b Marshall	16
B.C. Broad c Dujon b Marshall	1
M.D. Moxon run out	14
D.I. Gower c Richardson b Patterson	1
A.J. Lamb run out	113
D.R. Pringle lbw b Walsh	0
†P.R. Downton lbw b Marshall	27
*J.E. Emburey b Ambrose	30
G.C. Small c Richards b Marshall	7
P.W. Jarvis not out	29
G.R. Dilley c Richardson b Patterson	28
Extras (b5, lb 20, w 2, nb 14)	41
Total	**307**

Fall of wickets: 1-27, 2-29, 3-31, 4-104, 5-105, 6-161, 7-212, 8-232, 9-254

Bowling: Marshall 25-5-60-4; Patterson 21.5-2-100-2; Ambrose 20-1-75-1; Walsh 20-4-47-1

Umpires: K.E. Palmer and D.R. Shepherd

Man of the match: A.L. Logie

Result: West Indies won by 134 runs

Second Test
Lord's

Haynes (right) *can afford to grin as Moxon gets out of the way.* (Opposite) *Not so good this time, though, for Moxon has stood his ground and taken a fine, diving catch.*

the two sides into cruel perspective.

The last five West Indies wickets again went cheaply, but England were left to score 442 or, alternatively, to survive for the best part of two days. Broad, Gooch and Gower were gone for only 31 and with them all sense of reality faded. Moxon struggled for two hours, Lamb, his head on the chopping block, made a feisty century, his fourth against West Indies, and there were some lusty blows from Dilley and Jarvis on the final day after lunch. West Indies had seemed in no hurry, Richards conducting affairs as if bent on education rather than annihilation. The margin of 134 runs could, one felt, have been increased at any time.

Marshall, who took 10 wickets for 92, was no novelty, but the contributions of Logie and Dujon at no. 6 and no. 7, with 176 and 105 runs respectively in the match as against Pringle's 1 and Downton's 38, sealed England's fate. Whatever changes England needed to make at Old Trafford, an extra batsman would have to be one of them. Amongst the bowlers Small, rarely finding the requisite length or line, was a disappointment.

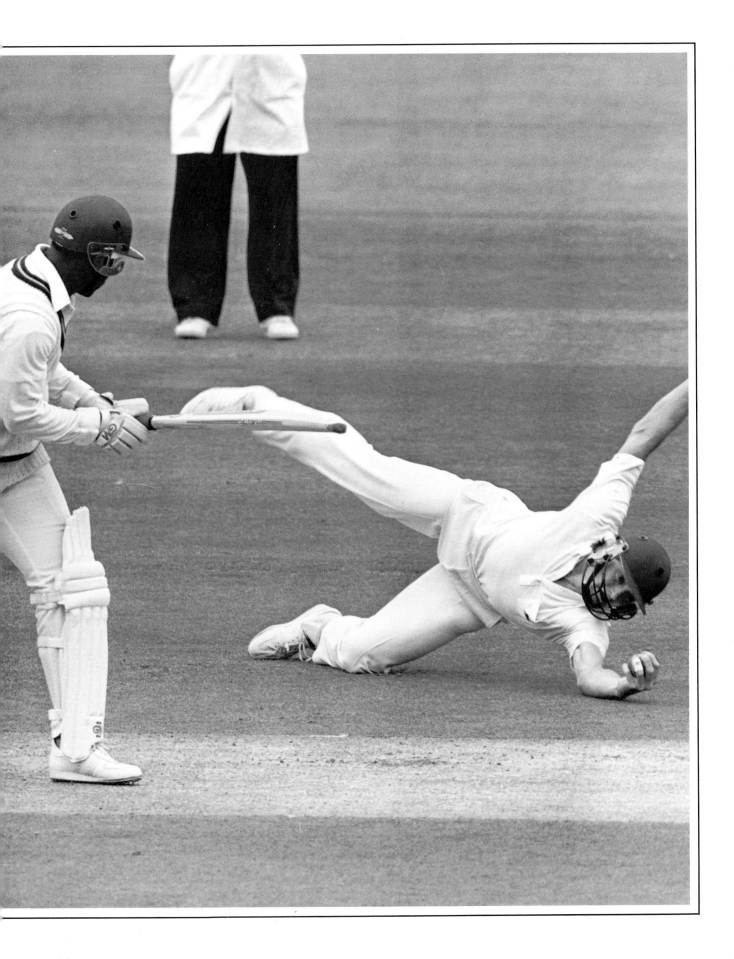

Second Test
Lord's

Gower (right) takes off in the gully and Ambrose will soon be bowling. This was one of England's better days in the field, and for once nothing worthwhile was put down in the slips.

Richards has played an unusually loose stroke during Dilley's purple patch and Downton takes his third catch of the morning. Dilley can rarely have bowled better than in his opening spell from the Nursery End.

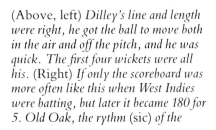

(Above, left) *Dilley's line and length were right, he got the ball to move both in the air and off the pitch, and he was quick. The first four wickets were all his.* (Right) *If only the scoreboard was more often like this when West Indies were batting, but later it became 180 for 5. Old Oak, the rythm (sic) of the* Caribbean, had done the trick. (Below) *Dilley, having taken 5 for 55, leads England off the field. Things seemed bright enough for them then, but next day the situation became as gloomy as the weather.*

Second Test
Lord's

(Right) *You may not like the idea but you've got to go! Broad is lbw for a duck and expresses his customary dismay. Gooch wants no part of it, and Marshall goes into a Bajan fling. (Below, left) Gooch does not usually kneel at work, but sometimes the situation and the unexpected behaviour of the ball demand it. (Below, right) Lamb, who looked in form, knows the worst. Marshall has got one to whip back at him and keep low into the bargain. (Opposite page) This is not a dance you often see at Lord's, and then only when England is batting.*

Second Test
Lord's

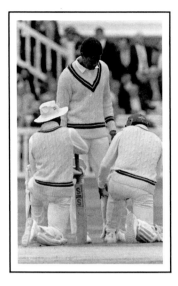

Richardson (above) is attended to by his dresser. He managed only 5 and 26, and at this stage of the season never really promised a long innings. (Right) Greenidge too had been out of runs, but now the sun came out for him and Richards, and both of them blazed away in their different fashions – Greenidge cutting and driving and pulling, Richards just being himself.

(Above) *Not a spare seat to be seen, and on the Saturday afternoon the Mound stand canopy gleamed in its full imperial glory.*

(Left) *Richards developed a strange fallibility this summer, several times making to cut balls too close to the wicket and dragging them on to his stumps. He and Greenidge put on 83 together and by the time both were out the match had gone beyond England's reach.*

Second Test
Lord's

In both West Indies innings, Dujon (right) and Logie (far right) shared handsome partnerships, 134 in the first, 131 in the second. Dujon with his relaxed, erect stance and Logie with his aggressive crouch took the battle to the bowlers, and runs streamed effortlessly from them.

(Below) For once it is Marshall's stumps that are flying, one of Jarvis' four wickets. Soon after this Marshall was back in action and England were 31 for 3.

Second Test
Lord's

Moxon had lasted for two hours, not achieving much but not often in trouble either, when this throw beat him. He looks in here, but the ball has hit the stumps and the bails must be off, though where they are is not clear.

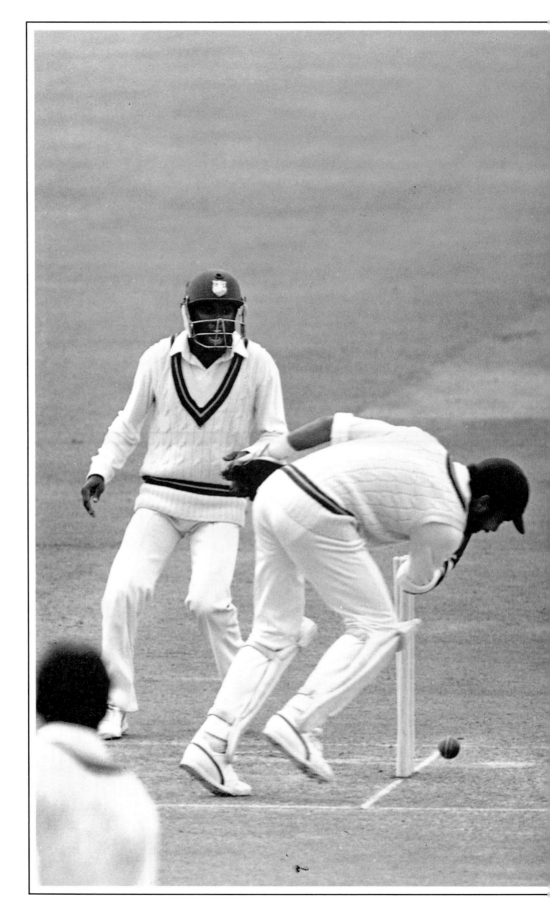

Second Test
Lord's

He glided in, arms and body sinewy and rolling, his legs accelerating. When he was bowling no batsman flourished or looked other than content to be at the other end. Meanwhile Marshall's returns were 6 for 32 and 4 for 60, nothing unusual for him.

(Far right, above) *Now, did I remember to turn the gas off? Lamb reflects during his second innings 113. His Test centuries tend to be during lost causes rather than match-winners.* (Below) *Emburey, after a flutter of bizarre strokes, takes a nasty one on his spinning finger from Ambrose and loses his wicket into the bargain. Slow bowlers, alas, have no means of redress against such indignities.*

Second Test
Lord's

Lamb (above), *in what would otherwise probably have been his last Test innings, acknowledges the applause for his hundred. It had been a long, long time since his last one, though he always suggested runs and in one-day matches generally produced them.*

(Above) *Patterson appeared anxious to decapitate Jarvis, but after some bold blows it was to Marshall's slower ball that Jarvis succumbed. In the calm of the match's closing overs he and Dilley put on 53 for the last wicket, but it was a gesture Richards indulged rather than a challenge.*

Steady on, you can't all be excused at once! Richards (right) has to plead with the players on the final afternoon to hang on just a bit longer and see the game out.

An appalling England

*Not a new form of glider being
wheeled into position, but the
usual depressing contraptions
so familiar to habitués of Old
Trafford.*

Of those who had played for England at Lord's, Small and Jarvis were apparently unfit; Broad, despite being warned about his visible displeasure at being given out and a total of one run for his two innings, was in the original thirteen but left out on the morning of the match. Gatting, after his frolic of runs in county cricket, returned and Capel replaced Pringle, on the basis of his batting rather than his bowling. DeFreitas was reinstated as replacement for Small and an extra spinner, the thirty-six-year-old Essex left-arm bowler John Childs, was given his first cap. The opportunity to blood a young batsman was not taken and England again chose a nominal all-rounder at no. 6, despite their poor performance at Lord's. For West Indies Haynes was out of action, so Richardson moved up to open and Harper came in at no. 7, his spin bowling an added benefit if Old Trafford played true to character. Benjamin replaced Patterson.

Emburey won the toss and quite correctly, in the circumstances, chose to bat. The pitch was on the sluggish side and the West Indies' bowlers settled for movement rather than lift.

They did not have to wait long for results. At 12 Moxon, not having scored, was bowled pushing out stiff-legged at Marshall, the ball going between bat and pad. Two runs later Gatting, heedless of his double fate at Lord's in 1984, played no stroke and was lbw. At 33 Gower was caught at third slip off Walsh, a familiar dismissal off a familiar stroke. When Gooch, who had seemed in no great discomfort, swished at a ball from Benjamin some way outside the off stump and got the thinnest of edges, the innings, and the match too, though only an hour or two old, seemed beyond recall. Altogether England lasted a mere sixty overs, during which scarcely a ball rose chest-high. Capel was bowled by a delivery from Benjamin that found him back rather than forward and Lamb, after a handsome pair of straight drives, was caught in the gully off Ambrose. The remainder went faint-heartedly through the usual motions and England, after a hold-up for rain, were all out for 135.

West Indies had fifteen minutes batting and off virtually the only ball Greenidge needed to play against Dilley he was dropped at second slip by Gooch, a comparatively easy catch at hip-height. Had this been taken England would at least have had something to show for the day.

The weather seemed intent on playing a hand, as if aware of the grotesque imbalance between the two sides. There were numerous interruptions and Richards, stuffing himself with pills, was nursing a fever. Childs, in an impressively relaxed and accurate spell, often had him bothered, but by the end of the day West Indies had reached 242 for 5, with Dujon and Harper well ensconced. Richards eventually despatched Childs for three fours and a six in quick succession, but he had been made to suffer in unusual fashion along the way. Both Richardson and Richards were out dragging balls outside the off stump on to their wickets, while Greenidge and Logie were lbw, to DeFreitas and Dilley respectively.

Held up by further rain and dismal light on either side of the weekend West Indies finally declared at 384 for 7, Dujon again batting with cool elegance and Harper stoically restraining himself for over five hours. Few balls got past the bat, even when Marshall was in.

England, starting their second innings 249 behind, lost the top three in the order for 60 before the end of the day. Marshall swung one in sharply to catch Gooch on the back foot, and then, having beaten Gatting with a brace of outswingers, had him caught at third slip. Gower was soon dropped at gully and Moxon at third slip, the light as distracting for the fielders as for the batsmen. Moxon did go soon afterwards, prodding at Benjamin's first ball and giving Richards the catch at first slip.

The weather forecast for the last day was such that England appeared unlikely to have to bat long to achieve a disgracefully undeserved draw. In fact they lasted less than an hour, 62 balls to be precise, the rain doing its bit to prolong matters. Seven wickets went down for 33 runs, 13 of these coming in three overs before a wicket fell. Gower had his usual flights of fancy and

performance

sometimes, if he survives these, he settles to better things. But his quick exit this time was almost cynical in its predictability – caught at third slip, where else? – and soon, after Capel was taken at silly mid-off, Downton and DeFreitas were caught there too. Ambrose, meanwhile, had found Lamb's glove. There was just time for Marshall to send Dilley's off stump flying in the old, familiar fashion before the heavens opened up and turned Old Trafford into a rice paddy. The figures mirrored on the waters were England all out 93, Marshall 7 for 22 in 15.4 overs.

It was difficult to remember a more appalling England performance in conditions that should have suited them and where fear was not an element. Henry Blofeld, analysing the technical failings of England's batsmen in the first innings in *The Independent*, observed that 'when survival is the best a batsman can hope for a runless frustration sets in'. But then how account for the same batsmen's ability to deal with the same bowlers in one-day cricket and the general run of county matches?

It seemed essential that, before Headingley, wholesale changes would have to be made but the noises from the management suggested otherwise. Gatting's return had been an anti-climax, Moxon confirmed that he was not quite of the quality, Gower looked to be lacking in *gravitas*, and Capel, whose bowling proved irrelevant, revealed that he was as yet far from being a Test match batsman.

During the weekend of the match Vivian Richards remarked, fairly dispassionately, that the middle of the wicket had been watered to lessen the bounce of the West Indies bowlers. He had no objection to this, but hoped that when West Indies produced wickets to suit their own bowlers no one would complain. The Lancashire secretary denied that there had been any directions to their groundsmen. Either way, it could scarcely have mattered less.

After the match two former England captains called for the resignation of the selectors, one of them, Ted Dexter, arguing that the committee as constituted was a waste of time and should be disbanded.

England won the toss

ENGLAND
First Innings

G.A. Gooch c Dujon b Benjamin	27
M.D. Moxon b Marshall	0
M.W. Gatting lbw b Marshall	0
D.I. Gower c Harper b Walsh	9
A.J. Lamb c Greenidge b Ambrose	33
D.J. Capel b Benjamin	1
†P.R. Downton c Greenidge b Walsh	24
★J.E. Emburey c Dujon b Walsh	1
P.A.J. DeFreitas c Greenidge b Ambrose	15
G.R. Dilley c Harper b Walsh	14
J.H. Childs not out	2
Extras (lb 4, nb 6)	9
Total	**135**

Fall of wickets: 1-12, 2-14, 3-33, 4-55, 5-61, 6-94, 7-98, 8-113, 9-123

Bowling: Marshall 12-5-19-2; Ambrose 17-5-35-2; Walsh 18.2-4-46-4; Benjamin 13-4-31-2

WEST INDIES
First Innings

C.G. Greenidge lbw b DeFreitas	45
R.B. Richardson b Dilley	23
C.L. Hooper lbw b Childs	15
★I.V.A. Richards b Capel	47
A.L. Logie lbw b Dilley	39
†P.J.L. Dujon c Capel b Dilley	67
R.A. Harper b Dilley	74
M.D. Marshall not out	43
C.E.L. Ambrose not out	7
Extras (lb 21, nb 3)	24
Total (for 7 dec.)	**384**

W.K.M. Benjamin and C.A. Walsh did not bat

Fall of wickets: 1-35, 2-77, 3-101, 4-175, 5-187, 6-281, 7-373

Bowling: Dilley 28.1-4-99-4; Emburey 25-7-54-0; DeFreitas 33-5-81-1; Capel 12-2-38-1; Childs 40-12-91-1

ENGLAND
Second Innings

G.A. Gooch lbw b Marshall	1
M.D. Moxon c Richards b Benjamin	15
M.W. Gatting c Richardson b Marshall	4
D.I. Gower c Richardson b Marshall	34
A.J. Lamb c Logie b Ambrose	9
D.J. Capel c sub b Marshall	0
†P.R. Downton c Harper b Marshall	6
★J.E. Emburey c Logie b Ambrose	8
P.A.J. DeFreitas c Harper b Marshall	0
G.R. Dilley b Marshall	4
J.H. Childs not out	0
Extras (b 1, lb 10, nb 1)	12
Total	**93**

Fall of wickets: 1-6, 2-22, 3-36, 4-73, 5-73, 6-73, 7-87, 8-87, 9-93

Bowling: Marshall 15.4-5-22-7; Ambrose 16-4-36-2; Walsh 4-1-10-0; Benjamin 4-1-6-1; Harper 2-1-4-0; Hooper 1-0-4-0

Umpires: D.J. Constant and N.T. Plews

Man of the match: M.D. Marshall

Result: West Indies won by an innings and 156 runs

Malcolm Marshall, having just taken 7 for 22, can put up with a little rain even if Tom Graveney cannot. Batsmen don't often face such a genial expression, but if you've been named Man of the Match you can afford a smile or two.

Third Test
Old Trafford

*Moxon b Marshall 0 (above).
The bat is straight enough but
there is a gap between bat and
pad and the ball has gone
through it.*

*Gatting plays no stroke and is lbw to Marshall.
Gooch turns away and everyone except the
umpire gives Gatting out. Soon he does, too.
Gatting's scores of 0 and 4 continued his bad
record against West Indies.*

Third Test
Old Trafford

Lamb looked England's best batsman at Lord's and Old Trafford; but here his favourite cut has found Greenidge in the gully and he is out for 33, England's top scorer all the same.

Dilley got into double figures, more than most of his colleagues managed, and it took the extended arm of the already extensive Harper reach to catch him. So England were all out for 135, Walsh with 4 for 46 having at last got a fair reward for his bowling.

Walsh can stretch higher than Ambrose, it seems (above), a contest Marshall sensibly avoids. They may be bigger than he is, but he knows they're no faster.

Third Test
Old Trafford

Childs had to wait until he was thirty-six to get a bowl in a Test match, but he soon got a wicket, Hooper being lbw. Childs had plenty of work to do, bowling 40 overs, but no more pickings came his way.

Richards seems to have missed this sweep at Childs, who initially caused him some trouble. Despite a feverish cold Richards still managed his usual assault, despatching Childs for three fours and a six, before dragging a ball from Capel on to his stumps.

Mushroom weather, but often though the heavens opened in aid of England's cause it needed only a pathetically small amount of play for England to be defeated.

Third Test
Old Trafford

It would not have been surprising if a whale had suddenly surfaced from beneath these drenched and billowing covers. Had England been able to make any sort of show they would have saved at least another two Tests because of interference from the weather.

Third Test
Old Trafford

Roger Harper may have mislaid his bowling action but he batted usefully, often with uncharacteristic restraint. In point of fact his bowling was not needed here.

Dujon never looked other than a batsman of class, his stance relaxed, his strokes cultivated. Of all the West Indian batsmen he and Logie came on most during the series.
(Below) This one has certainly gone up, but where is it coming down? Since Marshall remained unbeaten it probably went for six. All the West Indies bowlers appeared to relish their batting time whereas their English counterparts had the air of men going to the scaffold.

Third Test
Old Trafford

(Above) *At least, during Wimbledon week, there is something to look at while the water-hogs work – whether it is Gabriella Sabatini's legs or Edberg's whistling serve it is probably better than watching the grass grow.*

(Right) *Marshall looks rather open-chested here but, except for the inswinger, does not generally give that impression. Dickie Bird observed that Marshall went past him faster than any other bowler he had umpired to. It used to be said of the Derby winner Mill Reef that his feet were so light on the ground that it was as if a ghost had gone by. Similarly Marshall seems to quicken without effort, his legs a blur, scarcely bruising the turf.*

Gooch (above) has found
outswingers succeeded by one
that nips back to double him
up. Gatting too (below) *was
beaten by several that left him
before edging a straighter one to
Richardson at third slip.*

Third Test
Old Trafford

Moxon, having already been dropped at slip, was caught off Benjamin's first ball. Richards gave Benjamin surprisingly few overs here and at Headingley later, despite the fact that he was quick to take wickets at little cost.
(Above, right) Gower is caught at third slip again, the same sad story, endlessly repeated. He had made 34 but gave no feeling of sustained resistance.

(Opposite) Capel made 1 in the first innings but did less well in the second, when he was caught at silly mid-off by the substitute from Nevis, Arthurton, who was to take Greenidge's place in the side at Headingley.

Third Test
Old Trafford

Ambrose, continuing to get lift, hits Lamb on the glove and England now have nothing left to offer (above). (Right) Downton looks back apprehensively, but to the degree that England's slip catching declined so did the West Indies' improve. Harper, the best slip catcher on either side, makes no mistake; nor does he when DeFreitas (below right), without troubling the scorer, finds him a few balls later. Marshall was the bowler in each case, and he made it seem effortless.

Emburey (above) *usually manages to keep gully or the slips alert but this time Ambrose has got one to climb towards his chest and Logie, standing his ground, peers through his muzzle and catches him. Dilley (below) looks on his batting as something of a lark these days. He* plods in, waves his bat a time or two, and then, having been helplessly late in the stroke, loses his off stump. Usually he has to think about bowling but this time the match is over and he can go home.

New team - same story

(Above) *The question is rather whether Sir Len would want to come back. He had his share of short-pitched bowling forty years ago.* (Below) *The water-hog certainly has a more powerful jet than most. The groundsman looks a shade uneasy, as though people might think it had to do with him.*

After the humiliation at Old Trafford, and the fact that at Headingley an out-of-form spinner was not much of an asset, it was always on the cards that Emburey would be relieved of his duties as captain. He had led England in his two Tests perfectly well, except that he had failed to persuade his batsmen to make runs. In an interview with Norman Harris, published in the *Sunday Times* on 10 July, he observed: 'The West Indies are a young side but two or three of them happen to be two yards quicker than anything we've got. We always seemed to be forced on to the back foot and getting out bowled or lbw, whereas their batsmen are always looking to come forward against our bowlers. That's the whole difference in the pace attacks of the two sides'.

No-one would want to quarrel with that, nor with Emburey's complaint that most counties, in their obsession with 'result' pitches, make it impossible for batsmen to get into form between Tests.

After unusually prolonged discussions the team for Headingley proved not quite the wholesale sacking of the old guard as some had predicted. Emburey was replaced by Christopher Cowdrey, an enthusiastic and presently successful county captain, whose all-round skills were some way short of Test class, but who might just have been able to lift the spirits of his more senior and demoralised colleagues. Curtis, a consistent if rather stilted accumulator for Worcestershire, replaced Moxon, and Robin Smith, largely on the strength of a brief, aggressive innings a week earlier in the Benson & Hedges Final at Lord's, was introduced to add length to the batting. Athey, who must have thought his Test days were over, was brought back in Gatting's place – Gatting having declared himself a non-starter – and Pringle, despite his poor batting at Lord's, came in for Capel, though more as a bowler than all-rounder, since he was due to bat at no. 9. Downton gave way to Jack Richards behind the wicket. Gower hung on to his place by the skin of his teeth. Foster was at last fit again and came in for the disappointing DeFreitas. Only Gooch, Lamb and Dilley can have been sure of their places. The result was nominally stronger batting,

but a fairly pathetic attack which, if the weather turned out fine, would almost certainly have been ground into the dust.

At least one gamble came off and that was on the weather, which was consistently foul, play being repeatedly interrupted. When the sun did appear on the fourth day it was accompanied by gale-force winds. There was a novel happening on the first morning, odd even by Headingley standards, for after a delayed start and the bowling of only two overs a drain, blocked after a nocturnal deluge, caused some local flooding behind the stumps at the Rugby Stand end. Play, despite the activities of mobile water-hogs, could not restart until 2.30. West Indies must be used to these intrusions on the scheduled hours of play, but since they tend to need less than three days to rout England they appear to take them philosophically.

By the end of such play as there was England, having been put in, had reached 137 for 4, although at one stage they were 80 for 4. Gooch left at 14; Curtis, having lasted 94 minutes for 12, at 43; and Gower, after intimations that in this, his 100th Test, he would justify his presence, at 58. Gower's innings was like a catch in the breath or dazzle on water and as insubstantial, ending in the usual fashion. Athey looked correct and fluent, as he often does at the start of an innings, but he was seizing up when Ambrose had him lbw.

Lamb, batting with spirit and courage, was 45 at close of play. Smith, dropped at short-leg when he was 2, produced several fierce cuts to help Lamb add 57. There had been little in the pitch for the bowlers.

Next morning Lamb and Smith, by solid defence, mostly on the front foot, and robust strokes against everything short or overpitched, took their partnership to 103. They looked good for many more. Then, playing a square cut and starting on a single, Lamb tore a calf muscle, just about reaching the other end before subsiding in agony.

He can scarcely have got the pad off his one good leg when the scoreboard read 185 for 8 instead of 180 for 4. Cowdrey, Jack Richard and Pringle lasted 28 balls between them and were lucky to survive as long. Smith got a beauty from Ambrose, and Marshall and he, fairly ineffective hitherto, ripped through the remainder, exposing slow reactions and faulty techniques. So much for the attempt to reduce the tail.

West Indies began with their customary flourish, Dujon this time stroking and deflecting the ball as if he had been in all day. He made 13 off 14 balls and then sliced Dilley to cover-point. Hooper suggested another calculated, careful innings but after batting an hour was lbw to Foster. Richards, set on quick plunder, hit four boundaries in rapid succession. He then fastened on a long-hop from Foster only to find Curtis at square-leg flinging himself to his right and clutching the ball two-handed inches from the ground. Surprisingly, England were back in the match, even more so when Logie, who had been punching fours in all directions, mishit a slower ball from Pringle, who had just previously got past Haynes' rigid thrusts.

Saturday was another wretched day, West Indies, in the 24 overs bowled, advancing from 157 for 5 to 238 for 8. It should have been better than that from England's point of view, for Harper looked incredibly fortunate to escape being given out lbw before he had scored and two catches went down in the slips. Foster bowled well with no luck, Pringle earned his three wickets of the day, Dilley seemed out of sorts.

Monday was all sunshine and swirling winds and for an hour or so England promised to make a game of it. West Indies were eventually bowled out for 275, a lead of 74, and Gooch and Curtis knocked off 56 of these on either side of lunch. Then Curtis, having fended off a succession of steeply rising balls from Ambrose, was slow in adapting to two balls of full length, the second of which flattened his middle stump. Gooch reached a handsome fifty, but then edged a drive off Walsh and was securely held by Hooper at second slip.

This was at 80, and the virtual end of the match. At 83 Gower flicked Marshall so fine that Dujon scarcely had to stretch. Two runs later Athey, batting well, found one from Walsh that darted off the seam. Smith

West Indies won the toss
ENGLAND
First Innings
G.A. Gooch c Dujon b Marshall	9
T.S. Curtis lbw b Benjamin	12
C.W.J. Athey lbw b Ambrose	16
D.I. Gower c Dujon b Benjamin	13
A.J. Lamb retired hurt	64
R.A. Smith c Dujon b Ambrose	38
*C.S. Cowdrey lbw b Marshall	0
†C.J. Richards b Ambrose	2
D.R. Pringle c Dujon b Marshall	0
N.A. Foster not out	8
G.R. Dilley c Hooper b Ambrose	8
Extras (b1, lb 18, w 6, nb 6)	31
Total	**201**

Fall of wickets: 1-14, 2-23, 3-58, 4-80, 5-183, 6-183, 7-185, 8-185, 9-201
Bowling: Marshall 23-8-55-3; Ambrose 25.1-8-58-4; Benjamin 9-2-27-2; Walsh 12-4-42-0

WEST INDIES
First Innings
D.L. Haynes lbw b Pringle	54
†P.J.L. Dujon c Smith b Dilley	13
C.L. Hooper lbw b Foster	19
*I.V.A. Richards c Curtis b Foster	18
A.L. Logie c Foster b Pringle	44
K.L.T. Athurton c Richards b Pringle	27
R.A. Harper c Gower b Foster	56
M.D. Marshall c Gooch b Pringle	3
C.E.L. Ambrose lbw b Pringle	8
W.K. Benjamin run out	9
C.A. Walsh not out	9
Extras (lb 15)	15
Total	**275**

Fall of wickets: 1-15, 2-61, 3-97, 4-137, 5-156, 6-194, 7-210, 8-222, 9-245
Bowling: Dilley 20-5-59-1; Foster 32.2-6-98-3; Pringle 27-7-95-5; Cowdrey 2-0-8-0

ENGLAND
Second Innings
G.A. Gooch c Hooper b Walsh	50
T.S. Curtis b Ambrose	12
C.W.J. Athey c Dujon b Walsh	11
D.I. Gower c Dujon b Marshall	2
R.A. Smith lbw b Marshall	11
C.S. Cowdrey b Walsh	5
C.J. Richards b Ambrose	8
A.J. Lamb c Dujon b Ambrose	19
D.R. Pringle b Benjamin	3
N.A. Foster c Hooper b Benjamin	0
G.R. Dilley not out	2
Extras (b 3, lb 8, nb 4)	15
Total	**138**

Fall of wickets: 1-56, 2-80, 3-83, 4-85, 5-105, 6-105, 7-127, 8-132, 9-132
Bowling: Marshall 17-4-47-2; Ambrose 19.5-4-40-3; Walsh 20-9-38-3; Benjamin 5-4-2-2

WEST INDIES
Second Innings
D.L. Haynes not out	25
P.J.L. Dujon not out	40
Extras (lb 2)	2
Total (0 wkts)	**67**

Bowling: Dilley 4-0-16-0; Foster 7-1-36-0; Cowdrey 3.3-0-13-0

Umpires: H.D. Bird and D.R. Shepherd
Man of the match: C.E.L. Ambrose
Result: West Indies won by 10 wickets

Ted Dexter did not often look up to fast bowlers but he has to here. Curtley Ambrose, 'Man of the Match', has plenty of bottle, and a nice set of teeth too.

Fourth Test
Headingley

Well, I'll be jiggered! David Shepherd has seen some funny things in his time as umpire, but a flash flood in hot sunshine takes some beating.

was lbw to Marshall, Cowdrey was comprehensively bowled by Walsh, and Richards and Pringle equally so by Ambrose and Benjamin respectively. Lamb, in real discomfort and batting with a runner, struck a number of noble blows, as well as enduring uncomplainingly some uncharitably short deliveries from Ambrose. Ten wickets had fallen for 82 runs and England, all out 138, left West Indies needing no more than 65 to win. They got them, 27 overnight and the rest the next morning, without losing a wicket.

The bitter truth is that, while England have to bowl out every West Indies batsman, their bowlers simply and contemptuously brush aside England's middle and late order. What is more, in this match, they held the crucial catch at slip (from Gooch), Dujon picking up seven conventional ones on the way.

(Left) *Gooch held England together in match after match, but this time he went early, caught behind the wicket for 9, off Marshall.*

(Below) *Gower, in his 100th Test, dazzled briefly and then, in the familiar way, shuffled across to Benjamin and gave Dujon an easy catch. England, put in to bat, were 58 for 3.*

Fourth Test
Headingley

There are many positions that can be taken up when facing Curtley Ambrose, and here Robin Smith demonstrates a few of them. You can get well behind the line, feet earthed; let the ball fly harmlessly by, feet just off the ground; or weave backwards, body arched and feet dancing. In his first Test innings Smith, with 38, showed a welcome pugnaciousness and patience.

Fourth Test
Headingley

Lamb flashes Marshall past cover (right); Smith cuts Marshall for another boundary (below, left); and after a dreadful start, things begin to look almost rosy. 80 for 4 has become 180 for 4, and batting is looking quite enjoyable for a change, even if the weather is not up to Cape Town standard.

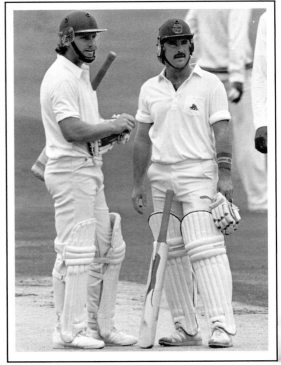

Alas, it was too good to be true. Lamb, pulling up after starting on a comfortable single, subsides in agony. He was batting at his best, making West Indies seem a bit short on ideas. He had scarcely got his pad off and returned to the pavilion when England were all out, the last five wickets going down for 18 runs.

Fourth Test
Headingley

Smith, deprived of Lamb's reassuring presence, went immediately afterwards. Ambrose, suddenly seeming a yard faster, produced a brute of a ball. Smith played many savage cuts and got resolutely forward in defence whenever possible.

(Opposite page) Marshall has to take off vertically to keep up with Ambrose. Arthurton is happy just to watch. Certainly this celebratory palming, much in evidence, is greatly preferable to the idiotic kissing, hugging and back-jumping once mandatory in English cricket and football.

Fourth Test
Headingley

There was not usually much visible of Gus Logie (above), *what with his helmet, muzzle, sweater and long sleeves; but he brought a brave heart to the West Indies middle order and a variety of punchy, aggressive strokes.*

(Opposite, top) *Harper could scarcely bowl a decent ball at the start of the session, but he* earned his place as a batsman and fielder, and in due course his bowling picked up and came in useful.

(Opposite, below) *Arthurton, a lone figure from Nevis, made a good start to his Test career, and in the covers was quick as lightning.*

Fourth Test
Headingley

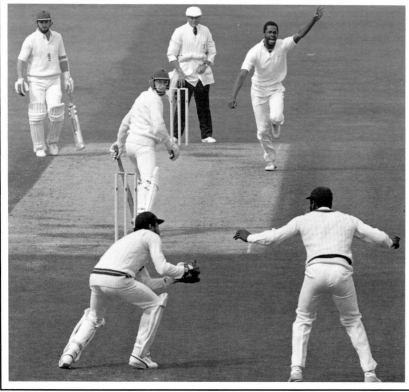

Curtis (top, left), softened up by some rib-ticklers from Ambrose, is late on a yorker and has an ugly mess made of his stumps. Not one to sell his wicket cheaply, he stayed some hours in his two innings but increasingly looked a batsman of limited resources. (Below, left) As often before, Athey set off in the manner of a high-class performer. But just when he ought to have been accelerating he seized up and then got out. Here Dujon catches him off a flier from Marshall.

(Above) *The end for Gower. He flicked at a ball pitching outside his legs and got the featheriest of touches. Dujon had not too much ground to cover, and he makes no mistakes with these.*

Fourth Test
Headingley

Benjamin (above) *was given less bowling by Richards than he seemed to warrant, his line, length and thrust being generally excellent. He finished with 4 for 29 in the match, bowling only fourteen overs altogether. One of his victims was Pringle (right), bowled here for 3 after making 0 in the first innings. The last five in the England order never delayed the West Indians for long.*

Haynes did not have the best of summers but, in the absence of Greenidge, he buckled down in the first innings after Dujon, Hooper and Richards had gone comparatively cheaply. He pushed forward over after over, head over the bat handle, occasionally unleashing a square cut. He did the same in the second innings to ensure West Indies a ten-wicket victory.

(Below) Dujon hits the winning run, making 40 of the 67 needed. No one gave more pleasure on either side as a batsman, and his wicket-keeping was immaculate. Some of his takes down the leg side at high speed were miraculous.

Fourth Test
Headingley

(Above) *Cowdrey could make little of Walsh and, having gone lbw to Marshall for 0 in the first innings, he was bowled by Walsh for 5 in the second. This delivery came back and hustled through low.*

(Opposite) *Lamb, coming in at no. 8, expected no mercy and got none, especially from Ambrose, who subjected the immobilised batsman to a series of bouncers. Nevertheless Lamb, in evident discomfort, batted more convincingly than everyone else except Gooch, and was second highest scorer with 19.*

The best pitch o

Gooch, captain in spite of himself, in comparatively genial mood. His duties seem to entertain him, to an extent that he might even be contemplating climbing aboard a Jumbo to India.

(Below) *The Oval produced a fine pitch and fine weather. The outlook for its future improved too. Next year The Oval could be blessed with new buildings and Aussie beer.*

There was a moment in the week before the fifth Test at The Oval when casualties outnumbered candidates. Christopher Cowdrey had to cry off with a bruised foot, and Kim Barnett, chosen for the first time, with a damaged hand. Athey, dropped but a possible replacement, was out for the season and Dilley had already withdrawn. Lamb, predictably, was some way off recovery from his pulled calf muscle. Bailey and Maynard came in to bat at nos. 3 and 5, with Gower dropped but Robin Smith retaining his place. The Oval had been the scene of several of Gower's most beguiling innings, but after a series of lack-lustre performances he had no cause for complaint. Jack Richards was lucky to keep his place behind the wicket and DeFreitas, recently demoted by his county for 'not trying', even more fortunate to come in for Dilley. Childs was preferred as the solitary spinner to Emburey, despite the latter's modest return to form for Middlesex. In the end the reluctant Gooch was persuaded to captain the side, a task he could well have taken on at Headingley.

In the best weather of the summer and on what proved to be the best pitch of the series England made a fair start, only for their innings to fall away in the familiar fashion. Ambrose struck a damaging blow early on, getting a straight ball to keep climbing up at Gooch, but Curtis and Bailey batted for over two hours each and Smith for well over three. At no time, despite the pace in the pitch and the fastish outfield, did any of them score fluently, but none of the West Indies bowlers strayed much in length, Ambrose, who took 3 for 31 in 20 overs, being particularly difficult to get away.

After Curtis and Bailey had put on 65 together, Bailey and Smith looked to be going even better. Then, in the last over before tea, Bailey was out, and it soon became clear that far from grinding out a score of 300 or so England would be lucky to get 200. Maynard, Richards and Pringle managed 4 runs between them. Capel and DeFreitas reached double figures but it was mainly through Robin Smith, last out for 57, that England reached 203 for 9 at close of play. Yet another promising situation had gone to waste. Harper bowled 21 overs of off-spin and took 3 for 50.

The next day, cloudless, and humming with heat and anticipation, looked the kind of one in which West Indies batsmen would revel. 270 for 3 seemed a fair forecast, but in fact, rocked on their heels by a wonderful opening spell from Foster, West Indies were bowled out in 59 overs for 183. The first four wickets fell for 57, all to Foster, and then, after the usual meaty partnership between Logie and Dujon, the last five for a mere 28, Pringle and Childs carrying on from where Foster left off. Logie played with his customary aggression for just over two hours, Dujon with expansiveness and charm for a shade longer.

At one stage, West Indies were 16 for 3. Haynes was caught behind off a Foster outswinger, Greenidge mishooked, and Richards, facing only his third ball, fended off his hip to Curtis at short-leg. Hooper hit an astonishing six off his back foot, but was then caught at slip. This was England's best

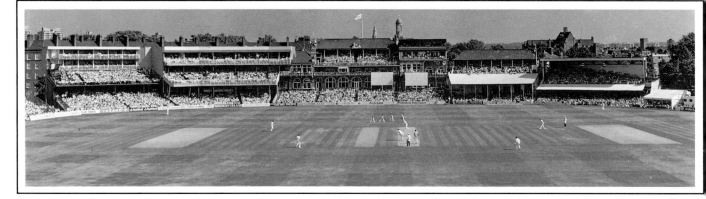

the series

bowling of the series, not only by Foster, who got varied movement off the pitch and attacked the off stump, but by Pringle and Childs in support.

England's lead of 22 was soon trebled by Gooch and Curtis, Gooch setting off with a satisfied flourish. However, hardly had a full house time to savour a score of 50 for 0 than all was brutally undone, 3 wickets falling for 5 runs. Curtis was lbw to Marshall, playing back, Bailey had his middle stump ripped out by Benjamin, and five balls later Smith, mistaking the swing, played no stroke and was lbw.

It depended on Gooch now, if he could find anyone to stay with him. Foster, the night-watchman, enjoyed himself the next morning, assuming most of the strike for over an hour and acquiring 34 runs. Maynard again lasted only a matter of minutes, and none of those that followed hinted they were good for either runs or tenure.

Gooch, becalmed and growing increasingly out of touch, remained, hour after long hour. In all he batted over seven hours for 84, but only for an over or two at a time could he exert anything like his normal authority. He was last out, having at one point in his forties spent an hour without scoring.

West Indies, therefore, were set 225 to win. By the end of Saturday they had made 71 of them, Greenidge surging to 53 not out, Haynes at a more dignified gait to 15 not out. Richards, suffering from a recurrence of haemorrhoid trouble, did not take the field, entrusting his duties to Greenidge, while by the evening England were being captained by Pringle, Gooch having split a

England won the toss
ENGLAND
First Innings

*G.A. Gooch c Logie b Ambrose		9
T.S. Curtis c Dujon b Benjamin		30
R.J. Bailey c Dujon b Ambrose		43
R.A. Smith c Harper b Marshall		57
M.P. Maynard c Dujon b Ambrose		3
D.J. Capel c Marshall b Harper		16
†C.J. Richards c Logie b Harper		0
D.R. Pringle c Dujon b Marshall		1
P.A.J. DeFreitas c Haynes b Harper		18
N.A. Foster c sub b Marshall		5
J.H. Childs not out		0
Extras (lb 6, nb 15)		21
Total		**205**

Fall of wickets: 1-12, 2-77, 3-116, 4-121, 5-160, 6-160, 7-165, 8-196, 9-198

Bowling: Marshall 24.3-3-64-3; Ambrose 20-6-31-3; Walsh 10-1-21-0; Benjamin 14-2-33-1; Harper 21-7-50-3; Hooper 1-1-0-0.

WEST INDIES
First Innings

C.G. Greenidge c DeFreitas b Foster		10
D.L. Haynes c Richards b Foster		2
C.L. Hooper c Gooch b Foster		11
*I.V.A. Richards c Curtis b Foster		0
A.L. Logie c Gooch b Foster		47
†P.J.L. Dujon lbw b Pringle		64
R.A. Harper run out		17
M.D. Marshall c and b Childs		0
C.E.L. Ambrose not out		17
W.K.M. Benjamin b Pringle		0
C.A. Walsh c DeFreitas b Pringle		5
Extras (lb 7, w 1, nb 2)		10
Total		**183**

Fall of wickets: 1-9, 2-16, 3-16, 4-57, 5-126, 6-155, 7-156, 8-167, 9-168

Bowling: Foster 16-2-64-5; DeFreitas 13-4-33-0; Pringle 16-4-45-3; Capel 7-0-21-0; Childs 6-1-13-1.

ENGLAND
Second Innings

*G.A. Gooch c Greenidge b Ambrose		84
T.S. Curtis lbw b Marshall		15
R.J. Bailey b Benjamin		3
R.A. Smith lbw b Benjamin		0
N.A. Foster c Logie b Benjamin		34
M.P. Maynard c and b Benjamin		10
D.J. Capel lbw b Walsh		12
†C.J. Richards c Dujon b Walsh		3
D.R. Pringle b Harper		8
P.A.J. DeFreitas c Haynes b Harper		0
J.H. Childs not out		0
Extras (b 3, lb 15, nb 15)		33
Total		**202**

Fall of wickets: 1-50, 2-55, 3-55, 4-108, 5-125, 6-139, 7-157, 8-175, 9-177

Bowling: Marshall 25-6-52-1; Ambrose 24.1-10-50-1; Benjamin 22-4-52-4; Walsh 12-5-21-2; Harper 6-3-9-2

WEST INDIES
Second Innings

C.G. Greenidge c Richards b Childs		77
D.L. Haynes not out		77
C.L. Hooper b Foster		23
A.L. Logie not out		38
Extras (b 2, lb 3, nb 6)		11
Total (2 wkts)		**226**

*I.V.A. Richards, †P.J.L. Dujon, R.A. Harper, M.D. Marshall, C.E.L. Ambrose, W.K.M. Benjamin and C.A. Walsh did not bat.

Fall of wickets: 1-131, 2-162

Bowling: Foster 18-3-52-1; DeFreitas 17-2-46-0; Childs 40-16-79-1; Pringle 13-4-24-0; Capel 3-0-20-0

Umpires: H.D. Bird and K.E. Palmer
Man of the match: P.J.L. Dujon
Result: West Indies won by 8 wickets
Men of the series: M.D. Marshall (West Indies)
G.A. Gooch (England)
Result of series: West Indies won the Wisden Trophy, 4-0

Fifth Test
The Oval

(Above) *Batsmen usually duck to bouncers but Bailey seems to believe in nodding them away as if he was a centre-forward.*

(Opposite page) *Robin Smith, on the other hand, hooked his first ball so ferociously that Dickie Bird enthusiastically signalled 'six'. He had to reduce this to 'four' on consultation, but it was a brave effort all round.*

finger on his left hand while fielding at slip.

There was some turn in the pitch for Childs, but Greenidge and Haynes carried on after the weekend without noticeable discomfort. Both were relentlessly correct in defence, courteous to Childs but dismissive of any lapses in length from the quicker bowlers. At lunch on Monday they had carried their partnership to 131, Haynes having been dropped behind the wicket off Childs when he was 37.

Greenidge was out to the first ball of the afternoon, Childs getting one to lift and turn. Haynes, unruffled, was again dropped behind the wicket during a fine spell by Pringle but Hooper was in no mood to progress by stealth. He was quickly down

the pitch to Childs, driving him for a four and a six, before dragging Foster on to his stumps. Logie also seemed reluctant to linger, and with Haynes safe in his hutch at the other end reeled off the necessary runs.

England were not disgraced, but while they struggled in both innings, West Indies a second time got proper value from the pitch, the circumstances and the weather. Gooch had a good match, as captain and batsman, Foster bowled at his best in the first innings, less well in the second, Pringle was never less than accurate and probing. Childs bowled 46 overs in encouraging conditions but though he was generally tidy and imaginative he never really suggested the match could be closely contested.

Fifth Test
The Oval

(Right) *When shall we three meet again? Well, the boot's on the other foot now, but Gatting looks happy enough, on the balcony but not, one hopes, on the shelf.*

(Below) *Bailey stuck it out for two hours, composed enough, and possibly suggesting better things. Then, in the last over before tea, Ambrose drew him into a stroke better unplayed and Dujon took the second of his four catches.*

(Opposite page) *Maynard lasted only a few moments, but none of them was uneventful. He was dropped, nearly run out, hit a full toss for his first runs in Test cricket, and was then caught, Dujon demonstrating how to take a catch at the fourth attempt.*

Fifth Test
The Oval

Jack Richards had an untidy match behind the stumps and made 0 and 3. Logie caught him here at short-leg, easily jumping twice his own height, a somewhat excessive gesture, perhaps, when the wicket was only Richards'. This was the second of Harper's three wickets and altogether he bowled 27 overs. Childs bowled 46 overs for England, so for once the spinners got some exercise.

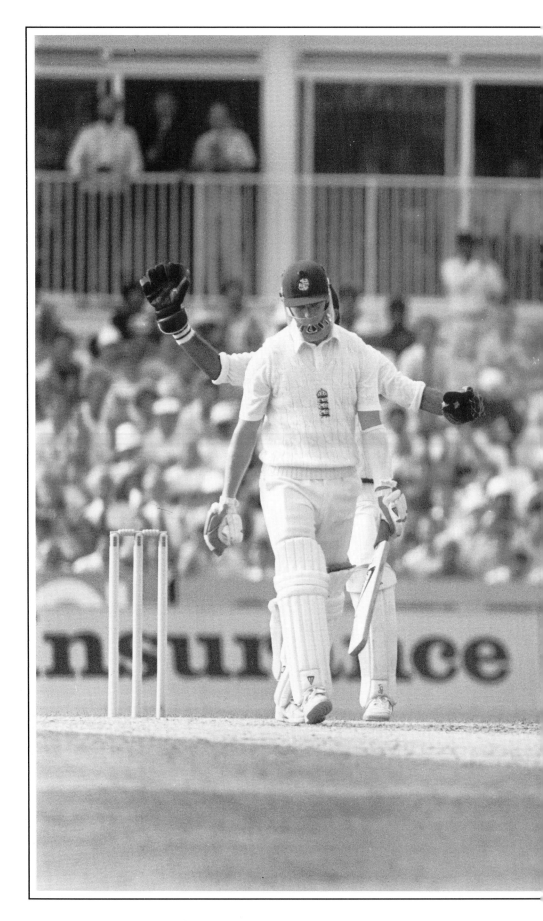

Fifth Test
The Oval

This (the Friday) was Foster's day. He took the first five West Indies wickets, and thoroughly deserved to have the ground named after him. When Haynes (top right) followed an outswinger West Indies had lost their first wicket at 9. (Above, centre) Richards was no sooner in than out. He fended down a shortish ball but Curtis was there at short-leg to scoop it up. (Right) With Richards' dismissal, Foster has the scoreboard worth looking at for once. The three wickets are all his, with two more to come.

Cornhill Insurance

1 2 3 4 5 6 7 8 9 10 11 Sub												LAST MAN	
Nº 3	TOTAL	Nº 5										0	
0 2	1 6	0 0										LAST WKT. 1 6	
WICKETS 3													
BOWLER 9		BOWLER 8									OVERS 9		
RUNS REQUIRED													
												7 8 OVERS REMAINING	
ENGLAND 1ST 205 2ND									BONUS		CT. 2		
WEST INDIES INNS		INNS							POINTS		B 9		

Fifth Test
The Oval

Dujon, Man of the Match, made 64, without ever seeming to exert himself. This stroke appears inelegant but it is unlikely it really was.

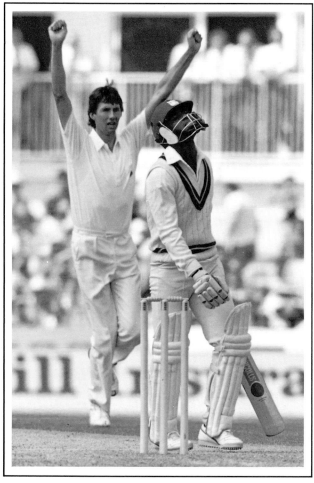

(Above) *The Milk Marketing Board sponsored several demonstrations of 'Kwik Cricket' during intervals. The players then had to cart the props away, some of them bigger than themselves.*

(Left) *Logie, as usual, got West Indies out of a hole, but Foster had him here, caught in the slips. Perhaps one of the bars got in the way.*

Fifth Test
The Oval

Robin Smith, in England's second innings, mistakes the swing, bows the knee to Benjamin and is given out lbw. He must have been watching Gatting. (Below) Foster, buoyant after his five wickets, set about the West Indian bowling as if he really was a no. 5, not the night-watchman. A hook got him out in the end, but he played some fine ones off Marshall, as well as several becoming off-drives.

(Opposite page) Gooch at his most Victorian and soldierly. This was a captain's innings, patient and protective, and it lasted seven hours. He was last out, his 84 being almost half England's total.

Fifth Test
The Oval

Pringle began to make runs once the Tests were over, but during them his batting was lamentable. Not surprisingly, perhaps, he attempted to commit hari-kari with his bat, but even that was unsuccessful.

DeFreitas (above) is caught and Haynes, the catcher, helps out the roller by doing a turn of his own on the pitch. DeFreitas had recently hit the fastest hundred of the season but there were no fireworks here.

(Left) Gooch does not usually send spectators to sleep, but he did not score for an hour, and sun after a spot of rum can bring on dreams of Caribbean beaches.

Fifth Test
The Oval

Childs rarely dropped short but when he did Greenidge (above) cut him as sharply as if he was attacking a wedding cake. In the first innings Greenidge had been out cheaply to Foster, but he was not going to let it happen twice. He tore into the bowling (below, right) and West Indies' task soon seemed negligible. Hooking Foster, he keeps bat and left leg in perfect alignment at the finish, a trick known only to himself.

(Below, left) Gooch would have done better not to get his hand to this at all, especially as it was a no-ball, for it opened a finger on his left hand and removed him from the fray. Pringle took over, acting as England's fifth captain of the series.

Fifth Test
The Oval

Haynes (top left) *has reason to grin, for he is on the way to 77 not out, having been dropped behind the wicket when he was less than half that. Hooper* (top right) *made 23 in his usual stylish fashion, and though he was bowled by Foster before the end it was of no account. Dujon and Logie rather stole his thunder as a batsman, but inevitably the runs will come.*

(Below) *With Richards in hospital Greenidge received the Wisden Trophy from Cornhill Assurance's Fred Dinmore. Not often can both captains have* been hors de combat on *the last day.*

(Opposite page) *London's West Indians acclaim their side's 4-0 victory. And, as Jack Bannister would say, why not?*

West Indian Summer

Malcolm Marshall. There was something altogether demonic about him, as if he had materialised out of nowhere. The most smooth, slithery, and elusive of bowlers, his physical presence gave no hint of the storms brewing.

POSTSCRIPT

Post-mortems were held throughout the summer, not just at the end. The usual explanations for England's failures were trotted out, scarcely varying: there was too much one-day cricket, too many overseas players, pitches had declined. Some saw a remedy in four-day county matches, a change advocated by many players, but not one enthused over by county members and secretaries. The simple truth, as far as the summer of 1988 was concerned, was that the West Indies, in all departments, were a class higher, able to raise their game whenever necessary. They were able to do without Patterson and Bishop for most of the time, and so accomplished a player as Arthurton could only get into the side when someone was injured. The austerity and economy of their bowling, with Marshall's slithery venom, Ambrose's gangling lift, Walsh's movement, and Benjamin's beady accuracy, made batting less an adventure than an undertaking. Harper, too, came increasingly into the picture, having already in the wake of Logie and Dujon helped to shore up the middle order. These three, in fact, led the averages with 49, 72 and 50 respectively.

The shoring-up was necessary, too, for England's bowlers, notably at Lord's and The Oval, had their golden moments against the earlier batsmen. Richardson was a disappointment and Hooper, after a dashing start to the series, rather faded. Both Greenidge and Haynes took some time to find their best form, and Richards, mercifully for England, was not often long on view. It was almost if he was content to appear, to fire off a few salvos, and then let the others get on with it. Had he needed, at any time, to produce a match-winning innings he would surely have done so.

At the beginning of June England, having won all the one-day internationals, had a potential batting order of Gooch, Broad, Gatting, Gower, and Lamb, with Moxon and Athey on the fringes. It did not seem to lack quality, but Broad dropped out of form and favour, Gatting self-destructed, and Gower, his fall from grace the saddest of all, played one undisciplined innings after another. Moxon and Athey were given their opportunities, but never got quite far

enough. Both look technically correct and assured players against any other bowling, but like those lower down the order, when beaten for pace always looked to be playing across the line.

By the time of the Oval Test only Gooch, who averaged 45 and Lamb, averaging 42, were still there. Curtis, Bailey, Robin Smith and Maynard had been blooded, their performances of varying auspiciousness but with modest result. Of the bowlers Dilley was not fit at the end, Foster unfit at the beginning. Jarvis and Small were suffering from something or other most of the time. Emburey did not suffer at all, but could neither take wickets nor make runs. DeFreitas seems to have lost both his batting and his bowling.

In retrospect, the dropping of Downton seemed a bad mistake. At this level he is a batsman of quite different stature to Jack Richards and, judging by Richards' clumsy work at The Oval in particular, a more reliable wicket-keeper.

The almost simultaneous injuries to Cowdrey and Barnett prevented, on the one hand, the perpetuation of a disastrous gamble and, on the other, the introduction of an unusually gifted and versatile character. His time must come.

Perhaps most cruel to reflect on, of anything, are certain batting averages: Gatting 9.50; Pringle 7.42; DeFreitas 7.20; Richards 3.25; Broad 17.75; Moxon 13.75. Of these only Pringle can be said to have earned his keep, but what on earth has happened to the handsome stroke player of those earlier days at Fenner's?

The coming winter in India, and next summer against the Australians, will set all this in sharper perspective. Is English cricket in a hopelessly bad state or is it merely that the West Indies, even in a transitional stage, are a case apart? Certainly, no other country seems to fare quite so poorly against them.

Nevertheless, watching English batsmen perform, even the most promising of the younger generation, is often a depressing experience. Curtis has guts and a good temperament, but his stiff, robot-like stance, bat aloft, does not argue natural ability. Bailey, shoulders stooped, reminds one too much of Tavaré, the bat dropped on the ball rather than freely swung to meet it, and little sense of pleasure communicated in the general deployment. Maynard, undoubtedly, suggests life and virtuosity, but there is at present a fidgetiness about him at the crease, not the perfect stillness of feet and head that all the great players have shown. Robin Smith looks to have what it takes, but there is a certain crudity about his methods, belligerence and beef rather than clarity of execution. Contrast all this with the upright, natural stance of Dujon and Hooper, the busy aggression of Logie. Or with the line of English middle-order batsmen from May, Colin Cowdrey, Dexter, Graveney, Parks, products of the same system. It is hard now to remember the way Bob Barber used to open an innings, or Peter Richardson, for example, both exuding confidence and delight in the game.

Almost certainly now, closer attention will be devoted to the proper preparation of pitches, especially if four-day county matches – so obviously successful during the early season experiment – become standard practice. But four-day matches on poor pitches will be no good at all. Gooch observed recently that travelling the counties in 1988 it was always with the expectation of having to bat on a minefield.

It would seem sensible for the registration of overseas players to be limited to one per county. It is probably true that the experience of English county cricket has done more to refine the techniques of younger West Indian, Australian, South African, New Zealand and Indian cricketers than it has been of benefit to the counties employing them. But players from abroad often give the impression of wanting to learn more and to enjoy the game more than their English counterparts. English cricket would be the duller for their absence, but you only have to look at the averages to see how they are hogging the scene.

Pre-eminence in cricket tends to go in cycles. England can scarcely sink lower than they have done these past few summers. It would be encouraging to think that present humiliation is the first step to a resurgence of spirit and achievement.

Graham Gooch. He may have expected minefields on the county circuit, but he scored plenty of runs. He was England's outstanding batsman and he and Allan Lamb were the only two whom one expected to make runs.

England v. West Indies
1988 Test Match Averages

ENGLAND

Batting

	Matches	Inn's	Runs	Highest score	Times not out	Average
G.A. Gooch	5	10	459	146	0	45.90
A.J. Lamb	4	8	254	113	2	42.33
D.I. Gower	4	8	211	88★	1	30.14
R.A. Smith	2	4	106	57	0	26.50
P.R. Downton	3	5	84	27	1	21.00
P.W. Jarvis	2	3	42	29★	1	21.00
B.C. Broad	2	4	71	54	0	17.75
T.S. Curtis	2	4	69	30	0	17.25
N.A. Foster	2	4	49	34	1	16.33
M.D. Moxon	2	4	55	26	0	13.75
G.R. Dilley	4	7	58	28	1	9.66
M.W. Gatting	2	4	38	29	0	9.50
J.E. Emburey	3	5	46	30	0	9.20
D.R. Pringle	4	7	52	39	0	7.42
D.J. Capel	2	4	29	16	0	7.25
P.A.J. DeFreitas	3	5	36	18	0	7.20
C.J. Richards	2	4	13	8	0	3.25
J.H. Childs	2	4	2	2★	4	—

Also batted: G.C. Small, 5★, 7; C.W.J. Athey, 16, 11;
C.S. Cowdrey, 0, 5; R.J. Bailey, 43, 3; M.P. Maynard, 3, 10.

Bowling

	Overs	Maidens	Runs	Wickets	Average
G.R. Dilley	136.1	26	403	15	26.87
N.A. Foster	73.2	12	250	9	27.78
D.R. Pringle	119.0	33	326	11	29.63
G.C. Small	37.5	6	140	4	35.00
P.W. Jarvis	57.1	6	217	6	36.17
J.H. Childs	86.0	29	183	3	61.00
J.E. Emburey	62.0	14	228	3	76.00
P.A.J. DeFreitas	92.0	16	253	3	84.33

Also bowled: D.J. Capel 22-2-79-1; C.S. Cowdrey 5.3-0-21-0.

Hundreds: G.A. Gooch, 146 (Trent Bridge); A.J. Lamb, 113
(Lord's).

WEST INDIES

Batting

	Matches	Inn's	Runs	Highest score	Times not out	Average
A.L. Logie	5	7	364	95★	2	72.80
P.J.L. Dujon	5	7	305	67	1	50.83
R.A. Harper	3	3	147	74	0	49.00
C.G. Greenidge	4	6	282	103	0	47.00
D.L. Haynes	4	7	235	77★	2	47.00
I.V.A. Richards	5	6	223	80	0	37.16
M.D. Marshall	5	6	135	72	1	27.00
C.L. Hooper	5	7	166	84	0	23.71
C.E.L. Ambrose	5	6	75	43	2	18.75
R.B. Richardson	3	4	71	26	0	17.75
C.A. Walsh	5	5	26	9★	3	13.00
W.K.M. Benjamin	3	2	9	9	0	4.50
B.P. Patterson	2	2	2	2	0	1.00

Also batted: K.L.T. Arthurton 27

Bowling

	Overs	Maidens	Runs	Wickets	Average
W.K.M. Benjamin	67.0	17	151	12	12.58
R.A. Harper	29.0	11	63	5	12.60
M.D. Marshall	203.1	49	443	35	12.65
C.E.L. Ambrose	203.1	53	473	22	21.50
C.A. Walsh	157.2	43	384	12	32.00
B.P. Patterson	74.5	13	270	4	67.50

Also bowled: C.L. Hooper 24-3-57-0; I.V.A. Richards 10-1-28-0.

Hundreds: C.G. Greenidge, 103 (Lord's).

England v. West Indies

Results: 1928-1988

MATCHES 95: ENGLAND 21; WEST INDIES 39; DRAWS 35

Of the 95 matches played between England and West Indies in the sixty years from 1928 to 1988, 54 matches have been played in England and 41 in the West Indies. England has won 14 in England and 7 in the West Indies; West Indies 24 and 15 respectively. Since 1963, when the Wisden Trophy was instituted, England has won 6 matches (the latest in 1973-74), and West Indies 29.

1928 – England, 3-0
1. England, inn & 58
2. England, inn & 30
3. England, inn & 71

1929-30 – England 1, West Indies 1
1. Draw
2. England, 167 runs
3. West Indies, 289 runs
4. Draw

1933 – England, 2-0
1. England, inn & 27
2. Draw
3. England, inn & 17

1934-35 – West Indies, 2-1
1. England, 4 wkts
2. West Indies, 217 runs
3. Draw
4. West Indies, inn & 161

1939 – England, 1-0
1. England, 8 wkts
2. Draw
3. Draw

1947-48 – West Indies, 2-0
1. Draw
2. Draw
3. West Indies, 7 wkts
4. West Indies, 10 wkts

1950 – West Indies, 3-1
1. England, 202 runs
2. West Indies, 326 runs
3. West Indies, 10 wkts
4. West Indies, inn & 56

1953-54 – England 2, West Indies 2
1. West Indies, 140 runs
2. West Indies, 181 runs
3. England, 9 wkts
4. Draw
5. England, 9 wkts

1957 – England, 3-0
1. Draw
2. England, inn & 36
3. Draw
4. England, inn & 5
5. England, inn & 237

1959-60 – England, 1-0
1. Draw
2. England, 256 runs
3. Draw
4. Draw
5. Draw

1963 – West Indies, 3-1
1. West Indies, 10 wkts
2. Draw
3. England, 217 runs
4. West Indies, 221 runs
5. West Indies, 8 wkts

1966 – West Indies, 3-1
1. West Indies, inn & 40
2. Draw
3. West Indies, 139 runs
4. West Indies, inn & 55
5. England, inn & 34

1967-68 – England, 1-0
1. Draw
2. Draw
3. Draw
4. England, 7 wkts
5. Draw

1969 – England, 2-0
1. England, 10 wkts
2. Draw
3. England, 30 runs

1973 – West Indies, 2-0
1. West Indies, 158 runs
2. Draw
3. West Indies, inn & 226

1973-74 – England 1, West Indies 1
1. West Indies, 7 wkts
2. Draw
3. Draw
4. Draw
5. England, 26 runs

1976 – West Indies, 3-0
1. Draw
2. Draw
3. West Indies, 425 runs
4. West Indies, 55 runs
5. West Indies, 231 runs

1980 – West Indies, 1-0
1. West Indies, 2 wkts
2. Draw
3. Draw
4. Draw
5. Draw

1980-81 – West Indies, 2-0
1. West Indies, inn & 79
2. cancelled
3. West Indies, 298 runs
4. Draw
5. Draw

1984 – West Indies, 5-0
1. West Indies, inn & 180
2. West Indies, 9 wkts
3. West Indies, 8 wkts
4. West Indies, inn & 64
5. West Indies, 172 runs

1985-86 – West Indies, 5-0
1. West Indies, 10 wkts
2. West Indies, 7 wkts
3. West Indies, inn & 30
4. West Indies, 10 wkts
5. West Indies, 240 runs

1988 – West Indies, 4-0
1. Draw
2. West Indies, 134 runs
3. West Indies, inn & 156
4. West Indies, 10 wkts
5. West Indies, 8 wkts